FRIENDLY GHOSTIES COLLECTION

'I loved all the ghosties' beautifully sketched characteristics, and the sensitive way in which King's story helps children understand fear: a "wibbly feeling in the tummy"'
Daily Telegraph

'King is very good at making children think about their world . . . hugely inventive and charmingly funny, early readers will adore having this book read to them and will love trying it themselves'
Literary Review

'Full of fun humour and ridiculous behaviour'
My Child

'Writer and illustrator have produced a hilarious fun-packed riot'

About the Author and Illustrator

Daren King studied in Bath and lives in London. *Mouse Noses on Toast*, his first book for children, won the Gold Nestlé Children's Prize. *Peter the Penguin Pioneer* was shortlisted for the Blue Peter Award. He is the author of four adult books. *Boxy an Star* was shortlisted for the Guardian First Book Award and longlisted for the Booker Prize.

David Roberts is the award-winning illustrator of over thirty titles. He has had a variety of interesting jobs, such as hair washer, shelf stacker and hat designer. He was born in Liverpool and now lives in London.

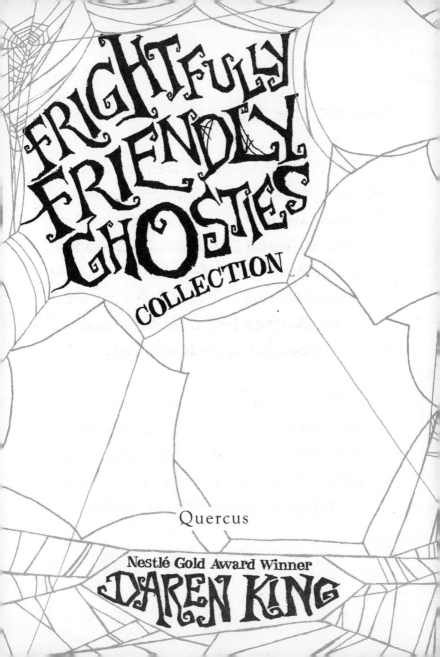

FRIGHTFULLY FRIENDLY GHOSTIES

COLLECTION

Quercus

Nestlé Gold Award Winner

DAREN KING

This collected edition first published in Great Britain in 2012 by

Quercus
55 Baker Street
7th Floor, South Block
London W1U 8EW

A CIP catalogue reference for this book is available
from the British Library

ISBN 978 1 78087 731 0

1 3 5 7 9 10 8 6 4 2

Printed and bound in Great Britain by Clays Ltd, St Ives plc.

For Rebecca

By Daren King for children

MOUSE NOSES ON TOAST

SENSIBLE HARE AND THE CASE OF CARROTS

PETER THE PENGUIN PIONEER

FRIGHTFULLY FRIENDLY GHOSTIES

FRIGHTFULLY FRIENDLY GHOSTIES:
GHOSTLY HOLLER-DAY

FRIGHTFULLY FRIENDLY GHOSTIES:
SCHOOL OF MEANIES

FRIGHTFULLY FRIENDLY GHOSTIES:
PHANTOM PIRATES

Contents

Frightfully Friendly Ghosties

Contents

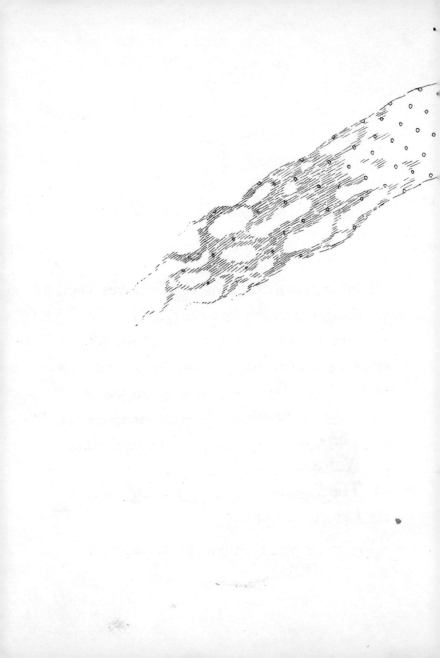

1
Pamela Fraidy

You still-alives are so mean to us ghosties. Only yesterday you locked Pamela Fraidy in the attic. She's a nervous wreck as it is! Not all ghosties can pass through walls, you know. That's only in cartoons and story books.

The only ghosty who can pass through walls is Charlie Vapour. He can pass through ceilings too, even when he's wearing a hat.

Poor Pamela. We could hear her shivering from outside the attic door.

'Try to keep calm,' I told her through the

wood. 'We'll get you out.'

'Help!' Pamela cried. 'It's d-d-dark in here, and I think it may be haunted.'

I asked Charlie to pass through into the attic, to comfort her.

'Certainly not, Tabitha,' said Charlie, in that adorable cockney accent of his. 'It would be an invasion of her privacy.'

'But she's petrified.'

'Who isn't? This rickety old house gives me the shivers. No wonder the still-alives always look flustered.'

'Charlie,' I said, 'please do comfort Pamela.'

Charlie passed his head through the door, then pulled it out quickly. 'It's dark in there. I reckon I'll wait out here with you, Tabitha.'

'But you're the only ghosty who can pass through.'

Once again, Charlie passed his head through the door, shuddered, and pulled it back out.

'Tabitha Tumbly, I refuse to float into that attic. There's a spider in there as big as my hat.'

Pamela was getting desperate. 'What are you *doing* out there?'

'Don't you worry about a thing,' I told her. 'We will float downstairs and fetch the key.'

That happened yesterday, and the key is still on the hook by the front door. The problem is, ghosties can't pick things up.

I can move things, I'm a poltergeist, that's why they call me Tabitha Tumbly. To be honest, I'm not very good at it. I can make a basket of laundry tumble off the sideboard, or an orange roll along the kitchen table, but I can't lift a key from a hook, float it upstairs and insert it into a keyhole. Only a still-alive can do that. But, as Wither would put it, you still-alives are mean.

Charlie Vapour

Charlie and I left Pamela Fraidy quivering in the attic and wisped downstairs to the hall, where we found Wither floating by the hat stand.

'Where are the still-alives when we need them?' Charlie asked him.

'The still-alives are frightfully mean,' said Wither, wrinkling his forehead. 'You're better off without them.'

'We need them to help us with the key,' I told him.

'They won't help,' said Charlie as the three of

us floated towards the front door. 'It was the still-alives who locked Pamela in the attic in the first place.'

'They didn't intend to.'

Wither folded his bony arms. 'Tabitha, they were being mean and you know it.'

'Even so,' I said, 'it doesn't hurt to ask.'

'There's a still-alive in here,' said Charlie, passing his head through the wall.

'I haven't been in that room since I was still alive,' I said. 'Which room is it?'

'It's the drawing room,' said Wither.

'The drawing room?'

'He means the lounge,' said Charlie. 'Wither is frightfully old-fashioned.'

'I call it the living room,' I said. 'At least, I did when I was still living.'

'Life was more civilised in my day,' said Charlie. He took off his hat – it's the polite thing to do – and passed through the lounge wall.

A moment later, we heard a loud
scream and Charlie reappeared,
white as a, um, ghost. 'Those
still-alives give me the
shivers.'

'Any luck?'

'No, Tabitha. There was
one sitting in an armchair
eating corn flakes. I bid her
good morning and she
picked up her breakfast tray
and threw it at me.'

'Perhaps she wasn't hungry.'

Wither frowned. 'Why are the still-alives so
mean?'

'I told you they wouldn't help,' said Charlie,
putting his hat back on. 'We'll have to move the
key ourselves. Tabitha, you can move objects.'

'Oh, not terribly well.'

'Don't be modest. You're a poltergeist.'

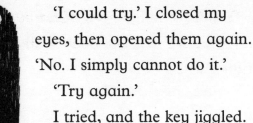

'I could try.' I closed my eyes, then opened them again. 'No. I simply cannot do it.'

'Try again.'

I tried, and the key jiggled. 'You must think I'm a frightful show-off.'

'Not at all,' said Charlie and Wither together.

'I'm sorry,' Wither said to Charlie, 'I didn't mean to talk over you.'

'No,' said Charlie, 'it was I who spoke over you. Tabitha, do try again.'

'Face the other way,' I said. 'I can't do it with you two watching.'

Charlie and Wither turned to the wall.

'No peeking.' I gave the key a good jiggle. It jiggled and jingled and jangled, but stubbornly refused to move from the hook.

'It isn't your fault,' said Wither.

8

'Don't blame yourself,' Charlie said, adjusting his tie. 'The hook is an awkward shape.'

3

Rusty Chains

We floated about for a bit, then Charlie had an idea. 'There is only one ghosty who can free the key from that hook, and that ghosty is Rusty Chains.'

Every ghosty has a ghostly ability. Rusty Chains has the ability to make things old and rusty. He also has the ability to bore a ghosty to tears. He drags these heavy chains around, so it takes him forever to do anything.

'I'll wisp away and find him,' said Wither.

'Charlie should go,' I said. 'He's the only ghosty who can pass through.'

'Not sure I can,' said Charlie, and he blushed bright white.

'You just passed through the lounge door.'

'It was a very thin door, Tabitha.'

'Charlie Vapour,' I said, 'this is no time for false modesty. Pamela is locked in the attic with a leggy spider, and we three are floating around doing nothing.'

Charlie adjusted his tie. 'Perhaps I shall pass through a teeny bit. Not enough to show off, just enough to find Rusty.'

Wither was losing his patience. 'Oh, get on with it!'

Charlie removed his hat – it's the polite thing to do – and poked his head through the tiled floor. 'Rusty? Coo-ee! Has any ghosty seen Rusty Chains? Ah, Rusty. Would you mind floating up here to help us?'

It took Rusty one hour to drag his chains up the cellar stairs and another hour to drag them

along the hallway to the front door.

'Is this it?' said Rusty Chains, eyeing the hook.

We nodded our ghostly heads.

'I can't do it now. I have to float back down to the cellar, then jangle my chains and moan a lot.'

Wither folded his bony arms. 'But it took you two hours to get here. How long does it take to

dab a bit of rust on a hook?'

'Anything for a quiet life,' moaned Rusty, rattling his chains noisily.

'Just the hook,' said Charlie. 'We don't want to damage the key.'

Rusty dabbed the hook with his rusty chains. The hook turned brown and crumbled to dust, and the key chinked onto the tiles.

'How did you keep the rust off the key?' asked Charlie.

'I didn't think about it. I just jangled my chains and moaned a lot.'

'You miserable old moaner!'

'Charlie,' said Wither, 'don't be mean. Rusty, we are grateful for your help.'

'Thank you, Rusty,' I said. 'Charlie, are you going to thank Rusty?'

Charlie removed his hat – it's the polite thing to do – replaced it on his head, and shook Rusty Chains by the hand.

4

Agatha Draught

'We're not out of the woods yet,' I said.

'No,' said Charlie. 'And Pamela Fraidy is still not out of the attic. She's probably been eaten by the leggy spider.'

'Spiders don't eat ghosties,' said Wither. 'Spiders are mean but they're not *that* mean. I will float upstairs and ask how she is.'

And off he wisped.

'We need to move the key along the hallway and up the stairs, Charlie,' I said.

'If we wait long enough, Tabitha, perhaps a still-alive will walk down the hall and kick the key to the foot of the staircase.'

I shook my haunted head. 'The still-alive is just as likely to hide the key in his pocket.'

'Can't you jiggle it across the floor?'

'I haven't the skills. What if I jiggle it wrong, and it floats out through the letterbox and jangles off up the street? Ah, here's Wither.'

'That was quick,' said Charlie.

'I bumped into Headless Lesley on the staircase,' said Wither. 'He'd just been up to the attic and held his head to the keyhole. It was too dark to see much, he said, but she seemed to be in good spirits.'

'Perhaps we should ask Agatha Draught,' said Charlie, toying with the brim of his trilby. 'She could create an eerie breeze and blow the key all the way to the foot of the staircase.'

'Poor Aggie,' said Wither. 'The still-alives are so mean to her. Have you seen the way they hunch their shoulders when she floats past?'

'When I last saw her,' I said, 'she was in the dining room. Let's float in and say hello.'

And off we wisped.

The dining-room door was open, so we floated straight in.

Three still-alives were sitting shivering at the dining table. Agatha Draught was floating behind their heads, blowing their hair without a care. When she saw us ghosties, she billowed the curtains for a bit then wisped over to say hello.

'Tabitha Tumbly, Wither, how the devil are you? Charlie, how lovely to see you.'

'This is no time for pleasantries,' said Charlie. 'Pamela Fraidy is locked in the attic with a leggy spider.'

'Poor Pamela!' gasped Agatha. 'What can we do-woo-whooo?'

On hearing Agatha's concerned cry, the still-alives leapt from their chairs and ran about. The two half-sized still-alives hid beneath the table, playing a game I suppose, and the still-alive with the high heels began to scream.

'Never mind them,' said Wither. 'They're just mean.'

'It's frightfully rude,' said Charlie as the four of us floated out to the hall. 'Agatha, will you help?'

'You could create a draught,' I said, 'and blow the key down the hall to the foot of the staircase.'

'We saw the way you billowed those curtains,' said Charlie. 'Awfully impressive.'

'You must think I'm the most ghastly show-off.'

'Not at all,' we all said together, then I apologised for talking over Charlie and Charlie apologised for talking over me, and then Wither apologised for talking over us both.

'Had I known you were watching,' said Agatha, clutching her pearls modestly, 'I would

have billowed with a little more discretion.'

We floated up the hall to the front door, to where the key lay on the tiles.

'This is frightfully embarrassing,' said Agatha.

'We're not watching,' I said, and the three of us turned to face the front door.

A moment later we heard a clatter, and when we turned round Agatha was blushing bright white and the key was at the far end of the hall, at the foot of the staircase.

Wither, Charlie and I clapped our haunted hands.

'It is a very *small* key,' said Agatha.

5

Gertrude Goo

'All we have to do now,' said Charlie Vapour, 'is get the key up the staircase, then up the three rickety steps to the attic door.'

We looked at the staircase, at the varnished banister and the plushly carpeted stairs. And suddenly it seemed that there were an awful lot of stairs, and that the top stair was teeteringly high.

'How many stairs are there, Tabitha?'

'I don't know, Charlie. At my school we used calculators.'

Wither frowned. 'Our maths teacher used to

whack our knuckles with a ruler. Thwack!'

'Wither had a classical education,' said Charlie.

'That is correct. Latin, Shakespeare, Dickens. We learnt by rote.'

I looked at Charlie. 'What does he mean, rote?'

'I don't know, Tabitha. At my school we learnt to tap dance.' He removed his hat – the polite thing to do – and performed an elegant little jig.

And that was when Gertrude Goo floated into view. 'While you three ghosties are making merry, poor Pamela Fraidy is locked in the attic. The leggy spider keeps scampering about, and she's a nervous wreck as it is.'

'We were counting the stairs,' Charlie told her.

'I know this house inside out. I clean it from bottom to top twice daily.' Gertrude tickled the banister with her gooey feather duster. 'There are twenty-six steps in this house. The front doorstep, the back doorstep, nine steps down to the cellar, twelve stairs here, and the three steps up to the attic door.'

When Gertrude was still alive, she worked at the house as a housekeeper. This is why she is so house proud. She spends most of the day straightening pictures and flicking her icky feather duster. The trouble is, she leaves a trail of glowing blue goo wherever she goes.

'How do we lift the key up twelve steps?' wondered Charlie.

'That's easy,' I said. 'We ask the still-alives to carry it up.'

'They won't help us,' said Wither, folding his bony arms. 'You know how mean they are, particularly the one with the beard.'

'We could drop it in one of these shoes,' said Charlie, admiring a pair of black leather brogues. 'The still-alive will put the shoes on and walk it up.'

I shook my head. 'The key would smell of wafty socks.'

'We could stick the key to the sole,' Charlie said, 'with Gertrude's goo.'

'We'd have to turn the shoe on its side.'

Wither rubbed his bristly chin. 'What if we apply the goo to the key, then wait for a still-alive to step on it?'

We all looked at Gertrude.

'Don't look at me,' said Gertrude, waving the duster, spraying goo onto the carpet, ceiling and walls. 'I don't have any goo. I'm awfully fastidious.' And she floated off up the hall to the front door.

'The house would be cleaner if she spent the day in bed,' whispered Charlie Vapour.

Wither pursed his lips. 'Don't be mean.'

'Ah, here comes a still-alive,' said Charlie as

we heard the click of high heels. 'Miss, would you mind awfully –'

The still-alive screamed and ran back into the lounge.

Wither's lip quivered. 'How can they be so mean?'

'I should have removed my hat,' said Charlie Vapour, and we agreed that that would have been the polite thing to do.

'If you don't mind,' said Gertrude, floating back along the hall towards us, 'I have to finish my chores. The house won't clean itself, you know.'

'Gertrude,' said Charlie, 'would you mind applying a dollop of goo –'

'Charlie,' I whispered, 'Gertrude prides herself on her cleanliness. She would never admit to making a mess. We will have to trick her.'

Charlie gave me a knowing wink. 'Gerty,' he said, taking off his hat, 'this key is frightfully

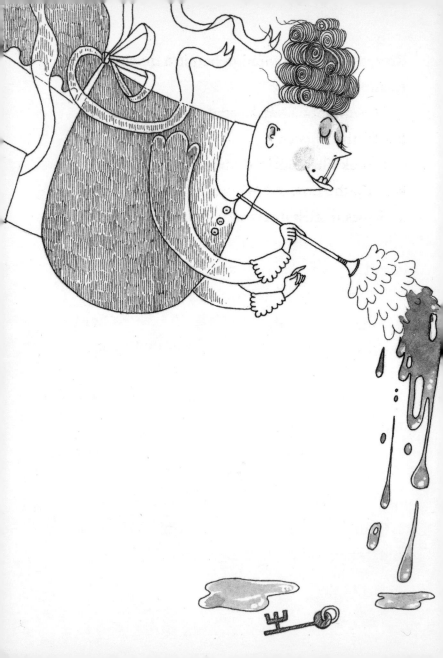

dusty. Would you mind giving it a quick spruce?'

'All in a day's work,' said Gertrude, waving her feather duster.

It took Gertrude ten minutes to polish that key. By the time she wisped off, the key was as sticky as a stick insect in a bag of sticky toffee.

6

Wither

We didn't have to wait long. The big beardy
still-alive walked out of the kitchen, a mug of
coffee in his hand, and stepped directly onto
the gooey key.

We floated up to the ceiling to hide. Myself,
Charlie Vapour and Wither.

'What if the still-alive doesn't walk up the
stairs?' Charlie said, adjusting his cufflinks.

The moment he said this, the still-alive
turned and went back into the kitchen,
slamming the door behind him, the key stuck
gooily to his shoe.

'Perhaps,' said Wither, 'he forgot the milk.'

'Or the sugar,' I said.

Charlie Vapour passed through the kitchen door, the show-off, then passed back. 'Yes, Tabitha, he's fetched himself a generous heap of sugar and he's giving it a stir.'

Wither frowned.

The kitchen door opened again and we floated up out of sight.

'I hope the still-alive walks upstairs,' I said.

We floated about for a bit, and Charlie dropped his hat – not a polite thing to do – but still the still-alive remained in the hall.

'Perhaps we could *ask* it to walk upstairs,' said Wither.

'Charlie,' I said, 'you ask. You have such frightfully good manners. Well, for a cockney.'

Charlie started to float down, but then he floated back up. 'Shall I remove my hat?'

'It's the polite thing to do,' I said.

And down he floated.

But then he floated back up. 'I don't want to appear too formal, you see.'

'It's good to be polite, Charlie.'

Again, Charlie floated down. This time, he wisped over to the still-alive and doffed his trilby. 'Awfully sorry to trouble you, and I hate to be a bother –'

'Please don't be mean to us,' said Wither, floating down behind him.

The still-alive yelped, threw the mug of coffee across the hall and ran up the staircase, the key still stuck to his shoe. 'Aaah!' he cried. 'Aaaaah!'

'How frightfully kind of you,' said Charlie, as we followed the still-alive up the staircase. 'We wouldn't have asked, only –'

'Help!'

'Pamela Fraidy is locked in the attic,' I said, 'with a leggy spider, and –'

'Oh please help me!'

'And spiders are mean and horrid,' Wither added, covering his eyes with his hands.

'Please, no!'

The key dropped from the shoe two steps from the top.

'Thanks awfully,' said Charlie Vapour.

The still-alive ran into a bedroom at the front of the house and slammed the door. Charlie passed through, then passed back. 'It must be frightfully cold in those rooms, Tabitha. He's shivering and shouting, and he's pulled the bedcovers right over his head.'

'Never mind that,' I said. 'We have to lift the key up the top two stairs, then up the three creaky wooden steps to the attic.'

Charlie adjusted his tie. 'You can do that, Tabitha Tumbly. You're the poltergeist.'

'Hardly,' I said. 'I can topple the odd bottle.'

'Don't be modest. We saw the way you jiggled the key. If you can jiggle it, you can lift it.'

'Not with you two watching.'

'We're not watching – are we, Wither?'

And the two ghosties turned to face the wall.

I was just about to lift the key when Pamela Fraidy shouted through the attic door. 'Will you get on with it? I'm locked in the attic with a leggy spider, and I'm a nervous wreck as it is.'

'Certainly,' I said. But then I heard a blub. 'Wither,' I said, touching him on the shoulder, 'whatever is the matter?'

'Oh, Tabitha! Why do ghosties have to be so mean?'

'No one is being mean, Wither.'

'Pamela told us off. I hate being told off.' Wither rubbed his eyes with his hands. 'Tabitha, will you ask Pamela to stop being mean?'

I floated up to the attic door and peered through the keyhole. 'Pamela? Pamela dear, are you still there? Have you been eaten by the leggy spider?'

'I'm here, Tabitha. Wither is right. There is no excuse for meanness.'

'You've been under a lot of pressure, Pamela.'

'It's just so frightfully dark in here, and what with the leggy spider –' I heard a faint, eerie sob. 'Tabitha, please apologise to Wither on my behalf.'

I floated back down the three rickety wooden steps and rejoined Wither and Charlie at the top of the staircase. 'Wither, Pamela says –'

'This key won't lift itself,' said Charlie Vapour.

'Face the wall,' I said, 'and I'll see what I can do.'

Charlie and Wither turned away. I lifted the key and fitted it into the lock.

7

Humphrey Bump

'You were marvellous, darling, marvellous,'
Charlie said, clapping his hands. 'We're awfully
impressed.'

'All I did was lift the key –'

'You fitted it into the lock, Tabitha. No other
ghosty could have done that.'

'Charlie, you can pass through walls.'

He shrugged. 'Bricks and mortar, Tabitha.'

'I can't do anything,' said Wither, and his
bottom lip trembled. 'All I do is blub and
tremble and flit about.'

'But you're in touch with your feelings,' I told him. 'What a wonderful quality to possess.'

'You should write poetry, Wither,' said Charlie, and he looked at me and winked.

'Actually, I do write poetry.'

'There,' I said. 'You *can* do something.'

'My poems won't get Pamela out of the attic.'

'You could write a poem about key-turning,' said Charlie.

'And how would that help?'

We heard Pamela Fraidy clear her throat. 'Er-herm! If you three wouldn't mind –'

'We'll have you out in the turn of a key,' said Charlie Vapour. 'Tabitha?'

'Avert your gaze, and I will see what I can do.'

'That's the spirit,' said Charlie Vapour. He turned to face the wall – the polite thing to do – and Wither buried his eyes in his bottom lip.

'It's no good,' I said, jiggling the key. 'I can turn the key but the door needs a push.'

'We could ask Humphrey Bump to bump into it,' said Charlie Vapour.

Humphrey is the sort of ghosty who can bump into still-alives, then wisp away the moment they turn round. He can bump into doors, furniture and household pets.

'That bumbling schoolboy won't help,' said Wither. 'You know how mean-spirited he is.'

'We could ask him nicely,' I said.

Wither bit his fingernails nervously. 'I could read him one of my poems, in payment.'

'That's a lovely idea,' I said. 'I saw him bobbing about in the back bedroom. Wither, do float in and fetch him.'

'I don't mean to be rude,' Charlie whispered as Wither wisped away, 'but Wither's poems are drivel.'

To our shivery surprise, when Wither floated out from the bedroom, Humphrey was floating beside him.

Humphrey wisped into position, and I gave the key a twist. But Humphrey just bobbed about, his hands in his blazer pockets. 'I can't do it with everybody watching.'

'Let's give the boy some privacy,' said Charlie. 'After all, it is the polite thing to do.' He adjusted his hat, then followed Wither into the back bedroom.

I turned the key, Humphrey bumped, the bolt unbolted, the attic door creaked open, and out wisped Pamela. 'Thank heavens for that!'

I shook Humphrey by the hand. 'Awfully kind of you to help.'

'I didn't have much choice,' Humphrey said. 'Wither threatened to read me one of his poems.'

8

The Attic

Humphrey pulled a ghostly lollipop from his pocket and offered it to Pamela Fraidy.

'I'm sweet enough as it is,' said Pamela, 'but thanks awfully.'

'How did you end up locked in the attic?' Humphrey asked.

'I floated in to say hello to one of the still-alives, the one with the adorable high heels. She was sorting through a box of crockery. She let out a frightful shriek, dashed out and slammed the door in my face.'

'Yes,' I said. 'I witnessed the whole thing. She

locked the attic door and ran downstairs with the key.'

'No wonder I'm a nervous wreck,' said Pamela. 'There's a spider in that attic as big as Charlie's hat. Perhaps we could stamp on it.'

Charlie looked horrified. 'Stamp on my trilby? You will do no such thing.'

'Not your hat, Charlie. The leggy spider. Or perhaps Humphrey could bump into it.'

Humphrey gave the lollipop a ghostly lick, then shook his head.

'You're a coward,' said Charlie, 'like Pamela.'

'That was double-means,' said Wither. 'You were mean to Pamela *and* you were mean to Humphrey.'

Charlie removed his hat. 'Pamela, please accept my sincere and hatless apology.'

'You have to apologise to Humphrey too,' said Wither. 'With your hat off.'

'He only wears that hat because he's going bald,' said Humphrey, giving the lollipop another lick.

'Will the meanness never end?' cried Wither, and he wisped down the staircase to the hall.

Pamela was deep in thought. 'I have an idea. Charlie, you could trap the leggy spider in your hat.'

'A spider in a trilby is still a spider,' said Charlie.

'Trap it in the hat, then tip the spider out of the window.'

'Worth a try,' Charlie said, 'but it's awfully dark in that attic. Tabitha, light the candle.'

'I'm not sure I have the skills, Charlie.'

'Tabitha, if you can't light that candle I'll eat my hat.'

I floated into the attic, lit the candle – it was nothing, really – and floated out. 'I couldn't see the spider. It must have scampered away.'

'Leave this to me,' Charlie said, adjusting his tie. He checked the floorboards, the wooden beams and the brickwork. The candle flickered and the wind howled, but there was no leggy spider to be found.

'I think it scampered in here,' said Pamela, and she wisped into the study.

The still-alive in the high heels was seated at the desk, typing on the clicky-clacky typewriter. When she saw Pamela, she screamed and ran out of the room, slamming the study door behind her.

'Oh, that's done it!' cried Charlie. 'We've only just rescued Pamela from the attic, and now she's shut in the study.'

'Can't Humphrey just bump the door open?' I said.

'Not a chance,' said Charlie. 'This door opens outwards.'

Wither came floating back up the staircase.

'The muse has struck. I have a poem in my head, and I just *have* to write it down. Where's my quivery quill?'

'In the study,' I said. 'With the leggy spider. And Pamela. One of the still-alives shut her in.'

'This really is the limit,' said Charlie Vapour.

'He's right,' I said. 'The still-alives have gone too far. Something must be done.'

We heard Pamela Fraidy's voice vibrate through the wood. 'You have to get me out. This room is far smaller than the attic. The leggy spider is scampering about, and I'm a nervous wreck as it is.'

'Pamela,' said Wither, floating close to the study door, 'I have an idea.'

We all wisped round to listen.

'I will dictate the poem through the door. Pamela, you will need quill, parchment and ink.'

9

The Larder

While Wither dictated his poem, Charlie floated off down the staircase, his trilby held thoughtfully to his chest.

I wanted to know where he was going, so I wisped down the stairs to join him. 'Charlie, where are you floating off to?'

'The larder, for a private think.'

'What about?'

'We need to call a meeting, Tabitha. I need to think of a time when we will all be together. Us ghosties are so frightfully busy.'

'I'll come with you.'

'I think better alone, Tabitha.'

'Me too,' I said.

Just as we were floating in through the kitchen door, Wither wisped down the staircase towards us. 'Where are you two floating off to?'

'The larder, for a private think,' Charlie said.

'Just the two of us,' I said. 'We think better alone.'

Wither pursed his lips. He looked like he was chewing a wasp. 'You don't want me around?'

Charlie shook his head.

'Well,' said Wither, 'as long as I know where I float.' And he floated off across the kitchen.

'Wither,' I said, floating after him, 'where are you going?'

'The larder.' He floated in through the larder door.

Charlie and I were about to float in after him when Humphrey Bump bobbed by. 'What are you three up to?'

'We're floating into the larder,' I told him, 'for a private think.'

'I'll join you,' Humphrey said, licking his lollipop.

'If you must,' said Wither, peering out from the larder. 'Though I have to say, we think better alone.'

Charlie was about to protest when we heard a rattling sound, followed by a low moan.

'It's coming from the larder,' said Humphrey.

'Rusty,' I said, floating in through the larder door, 'what are you doing here?'

'I want to be alone,' said Rusty Chains, and he gave his chains a good old rattle.

I was about to explain that the larder was a place for quiet contemplation when I heard a voice from above. It was Agatha Draught. 'How is a ghosty supposed to concentrate with all that rattling?'

'Agatha,' Charlie said, floating up to the larder ceiling, 'wisp out of here at once.'

'I'd rather not,' said Agatha, clutching her pearls. 'Gertrude and I are engaged in conversation.'

'That is, we were until you lot floated in,' Gertrude said.

'I came in here to be alone,' Charlie said, not removing his hat. 'All I want to do is float up and down, scratch the top of my head and think.'

'What about?' asked Agatha.

'We need to call a meeting. I need to think of a time when we will all be together. Us ghosties are so frightfully busy.'

'We're all together now,' Humphrey said, bobbing in through the larder door.

Charlie rubbed his chin. 'I rather suppose we are.'

'What is the meeting to be about?' asked Wither.

'The still-alives.'

Wither frowned. 'But they're mean!'

'That is what the meeting is about. Their mean behaviour, and how to stop it.'

'We could make friends with them,' I said. 'Then they won't be mean to us. No one is mean to their friends.'

'My friends are mean to me,' said Wither.

'I have invented three rules,' Charlie said. 'If we follow these three rules, the still-alives will like us, and they won't keep shutting Pamela in rooms.'

'Right,' I said. 'What's the first rule?'

'Every day, we say hello to the still-alives. It's the polite thing to do, and it will put the still-alives in a pleasant mood. The rule is called

Rule Three, because there are three rules. Any questions?'

Wither raised a pale hand. 'What's the second rule?'

'I was just coming to that. Each night, we tell the still-alives a bedtime story.'

'Everyone loves a good story,' said Agatha Draught. 'What is this second rule called?'

'It's called Rule One, because it is one of the rules. Is every ghosty with me on this?'

We nodded our haunted heads.

Wither raised his other hand. 'I don't wish to be mean, Charlie, but you promised three rules, and there appear to be only two. Is there a third rule?'

'I was just coming to that. No floating at night. It gives the still-alives the creeps. I have no idea why. We call this Rule Two, because there are two other rules.'

'I'm not sure that makes sense,' said Wither,

'but that's what we've come to expect from you, Charlie Vapour.'

Charlie folded his arms. 'Now who's being mean?'

10

Playing Cards

When we gathered in the hall the following day, Wither was dressed for bed. He was wearing blue-and-white striped pyjamas and a floppy nightcap.

Charlie laughed. 'Are you tired, Wither?'

'I thought we were doing Rule Three.'

'Rule Three,' I said, 'is the rule where we say hello to the still-alives.'

'That's right,' said Charlie. 'Are we all here? Ah, here's Gertrude and Aggie. Anyone heard from Rusty?'

'Had to cancel,' I said. 'Something about ten billion years in purgatory.'

'We can't wait that long. We'll have to start without him. Humphrey, would you mind awfully?'

Humphrey bumped the lounge door, it swung open, and we floated in.

Two still-alives, the beardy one and the one with the high heels, were seated at a card table, playing a game of cards.

I myself am terribly shy, but Charlie wisped up to them, bold as brass, took off his hat – the polite thing to do – and bid them a good day.

The still-alives were so surprised the beardy one dropped his cards and dived beneath the table, and the other dashed across the room and hid behind the curtains.

'Perhaps we should have knocked,' said Charlie Vapour.

'We came to say hello,' said Wither. 'We want

to make friends with you so you'll stop being mean.'

'Let me tidy these cards,' said Gertrude Goo, but all she could do was float above them, dripping a trail of glowing blue goo.

From under the table, the beardy still-alive screamed.

'Don't be cross with Gertrude,' said Charlie. 'She was trying to help. Humphrey, offer him a lick of your lollipop.'

Humphrey tried to float under the table, but he kept bumping into it, bump bump bump, until it toppled on to its side.

The still-alive rolled into a ball and pulled the rug over his head.

'The poor dear is shivering,' said Agatha breezily. 'It is cold in here, what with that open window.'

'Perhaps he wants us to play cards with him,' I said.

'I used to be a professional poker player,' said Charlie, 'when I was still alive. Who will deal? Tabitha?'

I dealt the cards as well as I could, but the deal turned into more of a shuffle. A mid-air shuffle. The cards ended up all over the carpet.

'Um, nothing up my sleeve,' I said, then floated off to the window, where the high-heeled still-alive had wrapped herself in the curtain. 'No need to be shy. I'm shy myself, but I don't let it bother me. Would you say so, Wither?'

'You're right,' said Wither, wisping across the room. 'Though you do talk to curtains, which is the first sign of madness.'

'I'm not talking to the curtain, I'm talking to the still-alive wrapped inside the curtain.'

'Oh, then you must lift the curtain so that the still-alive can hear.'

'I would, had I the skills.'

'Perhaps,' said Wither, 'we can ask Agatha to billow it.'

'Aggie?' I called, and across the room she wisped. 'Dear Aggie! That's the spirit. Terribly decent of you. Would you mind awfully?'

'Avert your gaze, then. Billowing makes one blush.'

Wither and I turned away, and Agatha blew up the most ferocious gale, and when we looked again the still-alive had gone.

'Oh dear,' said Agatha, clutching her pearls shamefully. 'I billowed too hard, and blew the still-alive out of the window.'

11
Bedtime Story

Wither kept his pyjamas on all day. 'There's no point dressing now,' he would say whenever a ghosty spookily sniggered. 'I'd just put on the second sock and it would be bedtime.'

We spent most of the day trying to free Pamela Fraidy from the study, but the door wouldn't budge. Poor Pamela. No wonder she's a nervous wreck.

When the still-alives went to bed, we gathered on the landing, and Charlie announced that it was time for Rule One. 'Are we all here? Still no sign of Rusty. Has anyone heard from Headless Lesley?'

'He has a headache,' said Humphrey. 'He dropped it.'

'Which rule is Rule One?' asked Gertrude Goo.

'Rule One,' I said, 'is the rule where we read the still-alives a bedtime story.'

'Everyone loves a good story,' said Agatha.

'Humphrey,' Charlie said, floating towards one of the front bedrooms, 'bump this door open and we'll get started.'

Humphrey bumped the door, and it opened with a creepy creak. The high-heeled still-alive was sitting at a desk, reading a book. She must have been terribly excited to see us. When we all floated in, her hair stood on end and she flapped her arms with joy.

'You can put the book away,' I said kindly. 'We're here to tell you a story.'

'Everyone loves a good story,' said Agatha.

The still-alive let out an excited scream.

'Calm down,' I told her. 'We haven't even started yet.'

'Once upon a time,' Charlie began, 'a still-alive was alone in a rickety old house. Rain lashed against the windows and the curtains billowed –'

'Like this,' said Agatha, billowing the curtains.

'– and six frightfully friendly ghosties wisped down the chimney and said hello,' Charlie went on, 'and those who were wearing hats took them off, like this.' And he removed his hat.

'It's the polite thing to do,' I said, in case the still-alive didn't know. Certainly she looked confused. She had her knees up to her chest and she covered her eyes with her hands.

'My nightcap stays on,' said Wither. 'I'm bald, Charlie. I get such a cold head.'

'Then,' Charlie continued, 'the ghosties danced around the still-alive in a spectral circle, like this.'

And there we were wisping around the room, faster and faster and faster, whoo-whooo-whooo, and I have to say, the still-alive was not impressed. She pulled her nightie up over her head and pressed her hands to her ears.

'I don't think it likes this story,' I said, wisping over to the bookcase. 'What kind of stories do you like?'

'Suggest a few titles,' said Charlie Vapour.

I began taking books from the shelf and showing them to the still-alive. I'm no better at suggesting books than I am at shuffling playing cards. The books ended up flying around the room.

'Perhaps the still-alive doesn't want a bedtime story,' said Wither, and the still-alive screamed.

'Everyone loves a good story,' said Agatha.

'Not this still-alive,' said Charlie, taking off his hat. 'Let's float away.'

'But I'm about to read the still-alive a poem,' said Wither.

'All the more reason to float away,' Charlie said, which was not terribly kind, you have to admit.

12

Striped Pyjamas

'I was the first ghosty here,' said Wither, when we gathered on the landing late that night. 'I was already in my pyjamas, you see. The rest of you had to wisp away and change.'

'Yes,' said Charlie, who was still wearing his trilby, 'and you have looked ridiculous all day as a result.'

Then we heard Pamela's shaky voice call out through the study door. 'I hope you're working on a rescue plan.'

'Pamela,' I called back, 'whenever we get you out, you get shut in again.'

'So you're leaving me in here forever? With the leggy spider? It's scampering about, and I'm a nervous wreck as it is.'

'We have to go to bed now, Pamela,' Charlie said. 'Goodnight.'

'But what about the rescue plan?'

'This is part of the rescue plan,' Charlie explained, doffing his trilby. 'If we make friends with the still-alives, they'll let you out as a gesture of goodwill. We'll retire to the bed in this room here, and let the still-alives get a good night's sleep. Humphrey, bump the door.'

The back bedroom was far grander than those at the front. When the door creaked open, we all gasped. The bedroom had an ornate four-poster bed and plush velvet curtains.

'I hope there's enough room for us all,' said Agatha Draught. 'Who will lift the sheets? Tabitha, you're a poltergeist. Would you mind awfully?'

'I don't have the skills, Agatha. Billow it with a force ten gale.'

'Tabitha dear, I'll be lucky if I can rustle up a gentle breeze.'

'Ladies,' said Charlie, taking off his hat, 'why not both try together?'

We both tried together.

The sheets lifted up, and bulged like the sail on a pirate ship.

'Well done, Tabitha,' said Agatha Draught, clutching her pearls joyfully.

'Agatha, I barely touched it.'

'Put your modesty aside,' Charlie said, adjusting his trilby, 'and come to bed.'

'I've not had a good night's sleep since I was still alive,' said Gertrude. She crawled into bed, leaving a trail of glowing blue goo.

Charlie floated into bed beside her, and Wither wisped in on Charlie's left and Humphrey to his right, and I floated into the space between Humphrey and Charlie, and then Humphrey bumped us all along to make space for dear Aggie. The blanket came to rest, covering our toes and knees.

'It's draughty here at the edge,' said Gertrude.

'You think it's draughty there?' I complained. 'You try lying beside Agatha.'

'Don't be mean to Agatha,' said Wither.

'What about me?' protested Humphrey. 'I'm at the edge, *and* I'm beside Agatha.'

'Wither has cold feet,' said Charlie Vapour.

'Don't be mean,' said Wither. 'At least I'm not wearing an outdoor hat.'

'Shh!' said Agatha. 'I can hear someone coming.'

Twelve eerie eyeballs turned to the door.

The door creaked open, and there, in striped pyjamas not unlike Wither's, stood the beardy still-alive.

'Perhaps he wants to sleep in this bed,' blubbed Wither.

'I should have thought of that,' whispered Charlie.

The still-alive didn't see us at first. He took a key from his pyjama pocket, closed and locked the door, and returned the key to his pocket. It was only as he crept across the rug that he noticed we were here, six grinning ghosties all in a row. He screamed a mean-spirited scream and ran back to the door.

'Awfully sorry,' said Agatha, clutching her pearls. 'We were trying to keep out of your way.'

'We can budge over if you like,' said Charlie. 'There's plenty of room for all.'

'We're trying to make friends with you,' I explained.

'Then you will stop being mean to us,' added Wither.

The still-alive pulled the key from his pocket

so excitedly that he dropped it onto the floorboards. He leapt up and down for a moment before diving under the bed, headfirst.

'He's trying to find the key,' I said. 'We should help. That's what friends are for.'

We all wisped under the bed.

'It's dark under here,' blubbed Wither.

There wasn't much room under the bed, so we had to keep wisping out and wisping back under again.

'Help! Help!' the still-alive yelled. Presumably he wanted us to help him find the key.

'It has to be here somewhere,' said Agatha, wisping in and out of the still-alive's pyjamas.

This went on for several minutes, until finally the still-alive crawled out from under the bed, grabbed the key from where it had rolled beneath the dresser, banged the door several times with his fists, wailed at the top of his lungs, unlocked the door and ran out.

Not frightfully friendly, I have to say, though he did leave the bedroom door open so we could float on to the landing and say goodnight to poor Pamela.

13
The Priest

Gertrude Goo and I were floating by the lounge ceiling when the doorbell donged.

'Who-woo-whooo could that be?' said Gertrude, dripping glowing blue goo onto the coffee table.

'Don't ask me,' I said. 'I don't even live here. I don't live anywhere. I'm not alive, you see.'

We floated to the lounge door and listened. First we heard the sound of high heels as one of the still-alives walked down the hall to open the front door. We heard voices for a moment, and then the footsteps again, click-click-click, together with the footsteps of the visitor, clump-clump-clump.

'I hope they don't come in here,' I said.

Gertrude agreed. 'Just look at the place. I'd better tidy up.'

I watched as Gertrude floated about the room, tidying pictures, ornaments, the vase of flowers and the rows and rows of books, spraying the room with glowing blue goo.

'That's quite enough tidying for one day,' I told her.

'I'll just give the shelves a quick dust. I'm terribly house proud, you see.'

The door handle turned with a creak.

'Gertrude, there isn't time.'

We floated up to the ceiling and wisped into the lampshade to hide. The still-alive entered with the guest, an elderly man dressed in black.

'He's got his shirt on back to front,' said Gertrude.

When the two still-alives saw the goo, their jaws dropped.

'I knew they'd be impressed,' said Gertrude. 'Tabitha, I do believe he's a priest.'

'There is something sinister going on,' I said. 'Let's tell the others.'

We wisped out of the lampshade, out into the hall and up the staircase to the landing.

Wither was dictating a poem to Pamela through the study door. 'When the other ghosties are mean to me, it makes my feelings sway like a tree.'

The moment he saw Gertrude and me floating behind him, he blushed bright white.

'This is only the first draft. And talking of draughts, has any ghosty seen Agatha?'

Pamela's voice vibrated through the wood. 'She's in the garden, floating by the washing line. I can see her through the window.'

'We'd better fetch her,' I said. 'Wither, the

still-alives have brought in a priest.'

'Perhaps,' said Wither, as we floated down the staircase, 'the still-alives have discovered religion.'

Charlie and Humphrey were floating by the stove, watching Agatha through the kitchen window.

'Agatha is drying the still-alives' laundry,' said Charlie Vapour, 'as a gesture of goodwill.'

'We must fetch her,' I said. 'The still-alives have brought in a priest.'

'A priest?' said Agatha, wisping in through the open window. 'We must say hello.'

'It's the polite thing to do,' said Charlie, lifting his hat.

And off we floated to the lounge.

The still-alives were there together now, the Priest, the still-alive with the beard, the still-alive with the high heels and the two half-sized still-alives. When we wisped in, they hid behind the sofa, all except for the Priest, who was engrossed in a leather-bound book.

'Perhaps they're planning a surprise party,' said Wither. 'They'll jump out and yell boo!'

'I didn't think priests liked parties,' said Charlie.

'Everyone loves a party,' said Agatha Draught.

The Priest ran his finger along the mantelpiece and wiped it on his handkerchief. He then reached into his trouser pocket and took out a wooden cross.

'What does the cross mean?' asked Humphrey.

'I think,' blubbed Wither, 'it means he's cross.'

The Priest held the cross in the air, half-closed his eyes, and muttered something we couldn't quite hear.

'He's trying to convert us to religion,' said Charlie.

'It's a bit late for that,' said Wither. 'We're dead.'

'Let's float in and explain,' I said, but as we floated in, the Priest reached into his other trouser pocket, took out a small white thing and waved it about.

'Garlic,' observed Charlie.

'I hate garlic,' said Wither. 'I liked it when I was still alive, but these days I find it abhorrent.'

'I don't think any of us ghosties like it,' I said.

We watched in horror as the Priest peeled the garlic bulb, separated it into cloves and placed them in different corners of the room.

'Garlic is related to the onion,' said Agatha. 'Did you know that, Wither?'

'Onion makes me blub.'

'Everything makes you blub,' said Charlie, and we floated out into the hall.

14

Wafty Garlic

'I don't like this one bit,' said Agatha Draught, floating by the lawn mower.

'It's our house too,' said Gertrude Goo.

'The entire house wafts of garlic,' said Wither, pinching his nose.

Pamela Fraidy wisped out of the study window and floated down to join us. 'Thank heavens for that,' she said. 'I thought they'd never let me out.'

'We'd forgotten about you,' said Humphrey,

bumping into the garden shed.

Wither gave him a withering look. 'Don't be mean to Pamela. She's been shut in the study since Tuesday.'

'With the leggy spider,' added Agatha. 'Pamela, how did you open the study window?'

'One of the still-alives opened it. She came in to fetch something, and I wisped into the typewriter to hide. It was the still-alive with the high heels.' Pamela rolled her eyes. 'Those shoes are to-die-for! She had another still-alive with her. He had his shirt on backwards. Must have dressed in the dark.'

'The Priest,' I said to the others knowingly.

'He placed garlic cloves around the room,' Pamela went on. 'Nailed an entire bulb to the door.'

'The meanness of it all!' cried Wither.

'I wouldn't have minded,' said Pamela, 'only, I can't stand the smell.'

'Garlic does tend to waft,' said Agatha, clutching her pearls.

'The still-alives don't like it much either,' said Pamela. 'That's why they opened the study window. Why put garlic in a study?'

'It's not just the study,' I said. 'They're placing it all around the house. Charlie has gone to investigate. We sent Charlie because he's the only ghosty who can pass through. Good old Charlie Vapour!'

'I wish I had a skill,' said Wither.

'You can write abysmal poems,' said Humphrey Bump.

'Oh, how mean!'

'I think your poems are delightful,' I said, though honestly, I thought they were drivel.

'I don't want to write poems,' said Wither. 'Who reads poems these days? I want to float through walls like Charlie, or blow leaves across the lawn like dear Agatha.'

'You can blub,' said Humphrey.

'Oh!' cried Wither, and he floated off for a blub.

'This is no time for blubbing,' I said. 'Here's Charlie.'

'That house wafts to high heaven. They've nailed garlic cloves to every door in the house.'

'Perhaps they're expecting vampires,' Wither said, floating back. 'Garlic wards off evil forces.'

'The leggy spider didn't seem to mind garlic,' said Pamela.

'Spiders don't have noses,' said Humphrey.

'Oh yes?' said Wither. 'Then how do they smell?'

Humphrey laughed. 'Terrible.'

Wither shook his head.

'Don't make jokes about spiders,' said Pamela. 'I'm a nervous wreck as it is, and now the house is riddled with garlic.'

'I could tidy it away,' offered Gertrude.

'Tabitha, you could float it out of the window,' said Charlie, adjusting his cufflinks.

'They've nailed it to the doors. I'm a poltergeist, not a carpenter. Have they opened any more windows?'

'Only the study window and the lounge,' Charlie said.

'How can the still-alives stand the waft?'

'They've put pegs on their noses, Tabitha. If only we could do that.'

'We can,' said Gertrude. 'I use ghostly clothes pegs to hang out the ghostly garters. And the spooky bloomers. Oh, and Wither's long johns.'

'Wither's long johns waft almost as much as the garlic,' said Humphrey Bump.

'Don't be mean to my long johns. If I don't wear long johns my knees knock.'

We floated about by the garden fence for a bit, feeling the breeze blow through our transparent bits, then Charlie had an idea.

'Our attempt at befriending the still-alives has failed. We need to get them out of the house. The only way to do that is to scare them out.'

'We can't scare the still-alives,' I told him. 'We're too friendly.'

Charlie adjusted his hat. 'Then there is only one thing for it. We call in a professional.'

15
The Ghoul

The following afternoon, Wither and I were floating about in the lounge when we heard a ghostly tap at the window.

'Who could that be?' I said, looking at Wither. My voice sounded odd because of the clothes peg.

'It could be the Ghoul,' said Wither. 'We hired one, remember?'

I peered out through the net curtains. 'I forgot we'd hired the Ghoul. This must be him. He's ugly enough.'

'Oh, don't be mean. Open the window, before

he gets cross.'

'I'm not sure I have the skills.'

'Try,' said Wither. 'Lift the latch.'

'Not with you watching.'

Wither covered his eyes with his haunted hands, and I gave the latch a jaunty jiggle. 'There. That's the best I can do.'

'Wait here, Tabitha. I'll float off and fetch Humphrey. Perhaps he can bump it.'

The moment Wither had gone, I flung the window wide open and invited the Ghoul inside.

A minute later, Wither returned with Humphrey Bump, followed by Charlie Vapour, Pamela Fraidy, Gertrude Goo and Agatha Draught, each with a peg on the nose.

'Would you like a clothes peg for your nose, Wither?' Gertrude asked.

'I can't smell a thing with this cold. Tabitha, how did you open the window?'

'One of the still-alives opened it. Everyone,

this is the Ghoul.'

'Hello, Ghoul,' said everyone.

The Ghoul chewed the tip of his nose, said nothing.

'This chap will scare the pants off those still-alives,' I said cheerfully.

Wither looked doubtful. 'But what about the Priest?'

'The Ghoul eats priests for breakfast.'

'And what about the Priest's wooden cross?'

'The Ghoul will use the Priest's wooden cross as a toothpick.'

'And the garlic?'

'We can take a holler-day,' suggested Agatha, clutching her pearls. 'When we float back, the garlic will have been eaten by rats.'

Charlie passed his head through the lounge door. 'I can hear footsteps.'

We all floated to the lounge door to listen.

First we heard the click-click-click of high

heels, followed by the clump-clump-clump of the Priest and the different-sounding footsteps of the two half-sized still-alives and the still-alive with the beard.

'Let's hide in the lampshade,' said Pamela.

'I'm not sharing a lampshade with the Ghoul,' said Wither. 'He might salivate on me.'

'And he's awfully big,' said Charlie. 'I think he's grown.'

Charlie was right. The Ghoul had been able to fit through the window. Now, the Ghoul was the size of a wardrobe.

'Let's wisp up out of the way,' said Agatha, 'and let the Ghoul get to work.'

'It's the polite thing to do,' said Charlie, and every ghosty floated up to the ceiling.

That is, every ghosty except for me. I wisped beneath the Ghoul's left eyelid. I wanted to get a Ghoul's eye view. And I have to say, the Ghoul put on quite a performance.

When the still-alives opened the lounge door, he bared his teeth, rolled his eyeballs, flared his nostrils, waggled his tongue, licked his lips, dribbled, and let out the most horrendous, horrifying howl.

The still-alives didn't like this one bit. Ghosties they could tolerate – after all, we're frightfully friendly – but a ghastly ghoul is quite different. All five ran down the hall to the front door. The high-heeled still-alive kicked off her shoes and ran barefoot into the street, followed by the two half-sized still-alives and the Priest. The beardy still-alive was the only still-alive who remained inside.

Ten minutes later, we heard a commotion from upstairs.

I wisped out of the Ghoul's eyelid and floated up the staircase, followed by Wither, and Charlie Vapour passed up through the ceiling.

The bearded still-alive was dashing from room to room, throwing clothes, toiletries and other oddments into a huge leather suitcase.

'He's off on holler-day,' said Charlie.

'No,' I said. 'Our plan has worked. The still-alives are moving out.'

'I hope they take the garlic with them,' said Wither.

'There's an open window in one of the front bedrooms,' I said. 'Let's wisp out and watch.'

The other ghosties were already outside, floating above the heads of the high-heeled still-alive, who had popped inside to fetch her shoes, and the two half-sized still-alives and several others who lived in the street.

Nothing happened for a minute or two. Then, the front door flew open and out tumbled the suitcase, followed by the still-alive with the beard and the ghastly Ghoul, who blew a raspberry and floated back into the house.

16
Leggy Spider

'That's that then,' I said, floating joyfully. 'The house is ours.'

'I wonder where the still-alives will live,' said Agatha. 'Perhaps they have relatives. An old lady in a felt hat, or a man who invents things.'

We floated down to the front door, which swung open on rusty hinges.

'Nothing can go wrong now,' said Wither.

But we'd only floated as far as the hall door when the Ghoul pulled such a mean-spirited face that we all floated backwards.

'Not like us to float backwards like that,' said Agatha.

'I didn't know we could,' I said.

'Perhaps,' said Charlie, 'the Ghoul made us jump.'

We all floated forwards again, but the Ghoul bared his teeth and once again we all floated back, further this time, to the front door.

'This doesn't feel right,' said Gertrude.

'I have goose pimples,' said Wither.

'And I,' said Agatha, 'have a wibbly feeling in my tummy.'

'I know that feeling,' said Pamela Fraidy. 'I get it all the time. It's fear.'

Wither folded his bony arms. 'You don't mean we're afraid of the Ghoul?'

'Impossible,' I said, but a moment later the Ghoul let out a horrific scream, and all seven of us wisped out the front door and up into the sky, and we didn't stop wisping until we reached the chimney pot.

Wither frowned. 'Pamela is right. We're afraid of the Ghoul.'

'Perhaps,' I said, 'this is how the still-alives feel when they see us ghosties.'

'That would explain their odd behaviour,' said Charlie.

'There's no excuse for meanness,' said Wither.

'But don't you see? The still-alives aren't being mean,' I told him. 'They run away because they're afraid.'

Wither gulped. I think he was swallowing a blub. 'So, what now, Tabitha?'

'We make friends with the Ghoul. Yes, we wisp down the chimney, say hello and wisp back up. This will put the Ghoul in a good mood, and he will want to be our friend.'

'And then he won't be mean to us?' said Wither hopefully.

I nodded. 'And then he won't be mean to us.

Who will go first?'

We looked at each other in spooky silence. A plane flew overhead. In the distance, a church bell chimed a spooky chime.

Charlie adjusted his cufflinks, his tie, his hat. 'I will go first, Tabitha. After all, it is the polite thing to do.' And off he wisped down the chimney.

I was about to say how brave he was, how noble and bold, and how he set an example to us all, when he wisped back up.

Agatha laughed. 'I have to say, Charlie, that was the fastest greeting in history.'

'I doubt he got as far as the fireplace,' said Wither.

'Do it again, Charlie. This time, I will watch through the window.' I wisped over the edge of the roof and floated down to the lounge window.

A moment later, Charlie floated out of the fireplace, his hat pulled down over his eyes, and

mouthed a hello to the Ghoul's back. By the time the Ghoul had turned around he'd wisped back up to the roof.

Humphrey Bump didn't do much better. A quick wave and he was back up the chimney, no doubt bumping the brickwork all the way.

The girls were next, Agatha Draught, who blew the Ghoul a kiss, and Gertrude Goo, followed by Wither, who hid his eyes in his top lip. 'Oh please, please don't be mean to me,' he blubbed.

When Pamela's turn came, she floated down the front of the house to join me at the window. 'Hello, Tabitha,' she said cheerfully.

'Hello,' I said.

Pamela floated up and down for a bit, the breeze blowing her creepy curls, then said, 'I thought I'd float down and say hello.'

'Hello,' I said.

Pamela looked up at the sky, at the wispy,

ghostly clouds. 'It's a lovely day, isn't it.'

'Yes,' I said. 'It's lovely.'

We floated about for a minute or so, then I looked Pamela in the eye and asked her if she was afraid.

'I'm not afraid, Tabitha. I'm petrified. I simply cannot say hello to that Ghoul.'

The other ghosties were peering down at us from the roof.

'You share my turn with me,' I said kindly.

Pamela smiled, somewhat bravely, I thought. 'All girls together!'

We held hands and floated in through the lounge window. When I turned round, there was no sign of Pamela. Then I heard a voice from behind the curtain.

'I can say hello better from behind here, Tabitha dear. I can wave, too. Though the Ghoul won't see, of course.'

The other ghosties – Wither, Charlie and

Humphrey, Gertrude and Agatha – had floated down to the window to watch.

'I guess it's up to me then,' I said to myself, then floated into the room.

The Ghoul was floating by the bookcase.

'Hello, Ghoul,' I said nervously. 'Do you remember me? I'm Tabitha. I hired you to frighten the still-alives, but you scared us ghosties too, by mistake.'

I waited. The Ghoul did not respond.

'Ghoul, listen. This has gone quite far enough. We own this house. At least, we do live here. It's our home. And we want you to leave. Immediately.'

The Ghoul said nothing.

A moment later, the house began to shake.

The books on the bookcase, the bookcase itself, the coffee cups on the coffee table, the vase of flowers, the pictures in their frames, the windows and doors, even the walls shook. They shook and they shook and they shook, and the foundations shuddered and juddered, until the bookcase fell with a terrific thud and the pictures flew from the walls and the glass coffee table shattered.

From behind the curtain, Pamela let out a frightened sob.

The Ghoul looked frightened, too.

'I can do this,' I said, 'because I'm a poltergeist. And if I can do this to the house, just think what I can do to you.'

And for a moment, I thought I had won.

But the Ghoul just laughed.

Pamela Fraidy floated out from behind the curtain. 'Is he in a good mood now, Tabitha?'

'I'm not sure. Pamela, I think we'd better –'

'Tabitha, you're right. Let's wisp out.'

The Ghoul had grown. His eyeballs were like watermelons, his teeth like chainsaws. His shoulders were now so wide they filled the room.

He opened his mouth and let out the loudest, most terrifying scream you could ever imagine. The sheer force sent Pamela and me sailing out of the window, and we found ourselves floating upside-down on the front lawn.

'I thought you floated in there to make friends?' said Wither. 'You were mean to the Ghoul and the Ghoul was mean to you.'

'You can talk, Wither,' said Charlie Vapour. 'You can't open your mouth without telling us off for being mean. And what could be more mean than that?'

'Ooh, don't be, um –'

'See?' Charlie said. 'Wither, you're the meanest ghosty of all.'

Poor Wither did not know which way to wisp. 'You, Charlie, are mean,' he blubbed, 'and you're mean too, Humphrey, and you three girl-ghosties are mean, and you're all frightfully mean and horrid, so boo snubs and utterly squash.' And he floated off into the house.

'Oh dear,' said Gertrude.

'You were rather mean to him, Charlie,' said Agatha.

Charlie adjusted his cufflinks, gazed down at the lawn.

'I'm worried about him now,' I said. 'In fact, I'm very worried, very worried indeed.'

'He'll be all right,' said Agatha. 'He'll mope for a bit and forget all about it.'

'That's not what I meant. Wither is in the house. With the Ghoul.'

'I'll float in and look for him,' said Charlie. 'It was my fault. And I'm the only ghosty who can pass through.'

'We'll all look for him,' I said. 'No need to float inside, Charlie. We can peer in through the windows.'

And off we wisped.

We checked the back of the house first, the

kitchen, the study and the back bedroom, and Gertrude wisped about by the shed. Charlie passed through into the bathroom, then passed back out, wearing the shower cap over the top of his trilby. But no Wither. We floated back over the roof and checked the front bedrooms and the lounge. And still there was no sign of Wither.

A minute later, the front door flew open and out came the Ghoul, floating off down the street as fast as he could, and I have to say he looked absolutely petrified.

We wondered what was chasing him at first.

It was Agatha who spotted it. 'Look!' she cried, as the Ghoul vaporised into the afternoon. 'The leggy spider.'

And there it was. The spider that had so unnerved us all. Not even Pamela was afraid of it now, and Pamela was, and still is, a nervous wreck.

'After meeting that big ugly Ghoul,' she told me, 'I don't think I'll ever be afraid of spiders again.'

Charlie threw his hat into the air and cheered with delight, and we all floated about on the lawn, laughing our spooky socks off.

'A colossal brute like him,' said Agatha, 'chased out of the house by a leggy spider!'

It was then that Wither floated out of the house.

'Wither,' I said, 'where have you been?'

'The larder, writing an apologetic poem.'

'Weren't you afraid of the Ghoul?'

'I felt too ashamed to be afraid, Tabitha. What are you all laughing at? And what happened to the Ghoul?'

'You were in such a bad mood,' said Charlie, 'you frightened him off.'

Wither pulled a face. 'The Ghoul was afraid of me?'

    Agatha and I exchanged looks. Agatha
shrugged.

    'That's right,' I said. 'That's what happened.'

    'You're our hero,' said Charlie. He shook
Wither by the hand, and we all agreed that this
was the polite thing to do.

Ghostly Holler-Day

Contents

1
The Postcard

If you had seen us ghosties gathered on the front lawn that morning, winter coats buttoned up to our glum faces, you'd have thought we were on our way to a funeral.

But then you'd have noticed the suitcases with Agatha's hat box on top like a cherry on a cake, and the penny would've dropped. Those ghosties are off on their holler-days.

I'm Charlie, by the way. Charlie Vapour. I take my hat off to you!

It all started yesterday evening, with Wither

hiding the postcard from Headless Leslie.

No, let me think—

It started with us lot floating about in the hall, bored out of our haunted heads. Tabitha had an idea, and the light bulb popped. That always happens when Tabitha has an idea.

Tabitha Tumbly is a poltergeist, see, and that means she can move things and make things happen, using the power of thought.

One minute you're wisping about in the glare of the chandelier or that antique lamp by the bookcase, and the next thing you know, Tabitha has one of her bright ideas and the room is plunged into darkness. And there's Pamela Fraidy trembling with fright and Wither blubbing about the price of light bulbs.

'What us ghosties need,' said Tabitha as we flitted about in the darkness, 'is a holler-day.'

'A holler-day?' I said. 'You mean, the sort you go on, then come back?'

'It usually works like that,' Tabitha said. 'A holler-day, by the sea.'

We all wisped into the light of the lounge.

'That is a super idea,' Agatha said, clutching her pearls. 'Every ghosty loves a holler-day.'

'And it's dead boring around here,' Humphrey Bump said, 'since the still-alives moved out.'

'But it's winter,' said Wither, gazing through

the lounge window at the blue-black sky. 'My knees will knock.'

'The sun always shines by the sea,' I told the daft old fool. 'At least, that's how I remember it, from when I was a boy.'

Agatha Draft floated over to the coffee table and grabbed a couple of holler-day brochures. 'Frighten-on-Sea, or Scare-borough?'

The trouble was, me, Pamela and Agatha fancied Scare-borough, and the other three favoured Frighten.

That was when we caught Wither hiding something behind the carriage clock on the mantelpiece. 'What have you got there?' I asked him, and he turned red – well, as red as you can get when you've been dead two hundred years – and wisped behind the clock.

'Why did he wisp behind the clock?' Humphrey asked me, loosening his school tie.

'He's embarrassed,' I told the boy. 'Wither

always wisps behind the clock when he's been
caught doing something he shouldn't.'

It took us ten minutes to get Wither out from
behind that clock. We tried everything.
Humphrey Bump bumped the clock with his fat

belly, and Tabitha jiggled the clock this way and that. I crossed my fingers behind my back and told Wither that if he came out, we'd let him perform one of his poems.

'Aggie,' Tabitha said, turning to Agatha Draft, 'you could rustle up one of your force ten gales, and blow him out.'

'I would,' Agatha said, 'if I had I the skills.'

'Rubbish,' I told her. 'If there's any ghosty who can blow Wither out from behind that carriage clock, it's you, Aggie.'

Agatha Draft possesses the ghostly ability to create an eerie breeze at will – the sort of breeze that ruffles a gentleman's collar, and makes the cat's fur stand on end.

'Look away, then,' Agatha said, and we all turned to the window while Agatha sent the clock sailing along the mantelpiece.

When Wither tumbled out, looking flustered and mixed up, he was holding this seaside postcard. GREETINGS FROM FRIGHTEN, it said on the front.

Humphrey snatched the postcard from Wither's bony, boneless fingers, blew a raspberry and handed the postcard to Tabitha.

'It's from Headless Leslie,' said Tabitha. 'Wither, this postcard is addressed to all of us. Why did you hide it behind the clock?'

The stubborn old fool refused to answer. He just floated by the fireplace with his hands in his trouser pockets, then wrinkled his brow in thought and said, 'Charlie, you told me that if I floated out from behind the clock, you would allow me to recite one of my poems. Well, here I am, and—'

'You didn't float out,' I said. 'Agatha had to blow you out.'

Tabitha handed Wither the postcard. 'You can read out Leslie's postcard instead.'

Wither floated over to the chandelier, and

tried to make out Leslie's spidery handwriting. He cleared his throat and started reading in that warbly, passionate voice he puts on when he recites poetry.

Humphrey stuffed his fingers in his ears and poked his tongue out.

'Normal voice, please,' Tabitha said. 'We can't make out a word you're saying.'

Leslie had written about how he'd gone on holler-day to Frighten, and how he had forgotten the way back.

'No wonder we haven't seen him since August,' Tabitha said.

'Headless Leslie would forget his head if it wasn't screwed on,' said Pamela.

'It isn't,' said Wither.

'But he wrote the address on the postcard,' I said, straightening my trilby hat. 'If he hadn't, it'd never have got here.'

'He must have forgotten the address after he

wrote it down,' Tabitha said. 'And perhaps he then tried to read it, but couldn't read the handwriting.'

'Leslie's handwriting is frightfully spidery,' said Pamela Fraidy, and she shivered.

Agatha floated about the lounge, rattling her pearls and fluttering her elegant eyelashes. 'Our decision has been made for us. We holler-day in Frighten, and find our dear friend Headless Leslie.'

'And his head,' said Wither. 'Don't forget his head.'

2
Wartime Ticket Office

So that's how it came about. A haunted holler-day by the sea, in the dead of winter.

Trouble was, we had to get there first, and we had an awful lot of luggage. And Humphrey Bump had this rubber ring around his waist – 'Just think of all the bumping you can do with that,' Agatha said – and he'd inflated it so big he could hardly fit through the front door.

Not only that, but us ghosties aren't terribly popular. Odd, really. After all, we're frightfully friendly.

It was too cold to be outside if you didn't have to, so there weren't a lot of villagers about. The only still-alive we passed was the batty old woman from down the road, who shook her walking stick at Pamela Fraidy and yelled something mean.

Poor Pamela. She's a nervous wreck as it is, and that old woman is enough to give anyone the shivers.

The moment we floated into the village train station, dragging our ghostly luggage, the ticket office door slammed shut and a CLOSED sign flapped into place behind the glass.

'This always happens when we try to buy train tickets,' said Wither, glancing at his pocket watch. 'Our sense of timing is atrocious.'

'There's always the old wartime ticket office,' I said with a wink.

'That ticket office was destroyed during the Blitz,' said Tabitha. 'I wasn't born back then, but my grandfather told me all about it.'

'Bombed out or not,' I said, 'it's still open, for those in the know.'

We flitted further down the track to where the train station used to be, and the air shimmered as the wartime ticket office materialised before our eyes.

There was a big hole in the roof and the windows had shattered, and there was a good deal of smoke, and when the station master floated out from under the counter he had his fingers in his ears, and his spectacles were speckled with dust and soot.

'Six terrifying tickets,' I told the man, doffing my hat.

'This ticket office is spiffing,' Agatha said. 'Is there a ghostly wartime train, too?'

'There is,' I said, 'but it's a steam train, so it's a bit on the slow side, if you know what I mean.'

'Trains should go super fast,' Humphrey said, bumping this way and that.

'The still-alives will make room for us on the still-alive train,' Tabitha said. 'They always do.'

'Only because they don't want to sit with us,' said Wither. 'You know how mean-spirited they are.'

3
Frighten-on-Sea

As we unloaded our luggage at Frighten Station, Pamela trembled with cold, Wither's teeth chattered and Agatha sneezed an eerie, breezy sneeze. I had to pull my hat right down to my pencil-thin moustache to keep the wind out of my eyeballs.

'Where is everybody?' said Pamela. There were no still-alives on the platform, and most of the passengers had left the train at Ghoole.

'It's November,' Pamela said. 'Who visits the seaside in winter?'

'A lot of people live in Frighten,' Tabitha said.

The handful of tourists who had braved the winter weather screamed at us and ran off, which ain't exactly friendly, you have to admit.

'This place is like a ghost town,' said Wither as we floated onto the main street.

'I expect they're all on the beach,' Agatha said. 'Winter it may be, but us ghosties are on our holler-days, and I intend to make the most of it.' She lifted the lid from her hat box and placed an elegant floppy sunhat on her head.

'My arms are tired,' said Pamela Fraidy. 'Charlie, Wither, sorry to be a frightful bore, but if you two ghosties were gentlemen you would offer to carry our cases.'

'Yes, of course,' I said, sort of polite but

miffed at the same time.

The three girl-ghosties dropped their luggage and skipped off into the chilly air.

'I'm too old and angular for luggage,' Wither said, flexing his bony arms. 'Charlie, you and Humphrey can carry it. I'm a poet, not a carthorse. I'd put my back out, and—'

'And I'm too dapper,' I said, adjusting my cufflinks. 'Humphrey's good at carrying luggage.' Before Humphrey could protest, I loaded him up with the six ghostly suitcases, Agatha's hat box and Pamela's bucket and spade.

'Tabitha, you must be frightfully cold in that bikini,' Pamela said.

'Not at all,' Tabitha said, rubbing her goose-pimply arms.

'The sea air is bracing,'

Agatha gasped as we turned onto the promenade. 'And – oh – I do believe it has stolen my hat.'

A winter gale had blown in from across the sea, tossing the waves this way and that, whistling through Wither's bony head, in one ear and out the other, and the wind had snatched Agatha's floppy sunhat and wisped it away.

I had to laugh. Well, she did look a sight, chasing after it down the prom-tiddly-om-pom-pom. And of course, Agatha being the breezy sort, she couldn't help but rustle up a breeze of her own. The closer she got to the sunhat the further along the promenade it blew.

'Don't just float there,' Agatha yelled. 'Float over here and help.'

The sunhat didn't stop tossing and tumbling until it walloped into a tatty old newsstand, situated on the edge of the beach. Agatha retrieved it from a pile of crumpled newspapers and blew dust from the floppy brim.

As Tabitha, Wither, Pamela and myself floated over, a group of tourists flung their buckets and spades into the air and ran off down the street.

'Why are you all leaving?' Wither asked them. 'Is it something we said?'

'Ghosts!' one of the tourists screamed back as they disappeared out of sight.

'I think they may be right,' Tabitha whispered into my ear. She was studying the headlines on the newsstand. 'It seems Frighten-on-Sea is haunted.'

FRIGHTEN PIER HAUNTED BY HEADLESS GHOST, the headline read.

'Don't tell poor Pamela,' said Agatha, arranging her sunhat. 'Ghosts terrify her, and she's a nervous wreck as it is.'

'Don't tell me what?' Pamela Fraidy said

with eyes like teacups.

It was myself, Charlie Vapour esquire – I take my hat off to you – who pointed out the obvious. 'The headless ghost is our Leslie.'

'Headless Leslie wouldn't haunt,' said Agatha. 'He may have been dead since Elizabethan times, but he's frightfully sweet, and it's hardly his fault his head comes off.'

A hackney carriage pulled up, led by a transparent horse. It was the sort of transport they'd have had in Frighten before I was born, back in Wither's time. The roof was loaded up with luggage. Humphrey Bump sat perched at the very top, stuffing his big round head with doughnuts.

'The hotel on Starfish Street,' I told the driver as I sat with the girls in the carriage. I closed the door and fastened the ghostly latch.

'This is frightfully fun,' Agatha said as the carriage lurched forward. 'I say, where's Wither?'

'Hither,' said Wither, and in through the window he wisped.

4
The Caped Figure

All that talk of hauntings gave me the shivers. I couldn't sleep that night, and after an hour of tossing and turning I decided to float out for a lungful of fresh air.

At least, that was what I told Wither.

The daft old fool was snoring his head off in the top bunk – Humphrey tends to go bump in the night, so we gave him a double bed to himself in the next room, and the girls shared a room across the hall – but of course, the moment my big toe touched the carpet he woke up.

Truth is, I had a spot of business to attend to. Wink-wink, nudge-nudge, say no more.

I floated into my comfy slippers, tied the cord of my dressing gown, then wisped under the bedroom door and down the dimly lit hallway to the back of the hotel, where I passed through the outer wall.

That's this little trick of mine.

Every ghosty has a ghostly skill, as I've said. There's Wither's ability to write the most dreadful poetry, and Humphrey's ability to bump into everything in sight, for example.

Well, I'm the only ghosty with the talent to pass through walls, ceilings and floors, even when wearing a hat.

Though I have to say, normally I remove the trilby when I pass through. After all, it is the polite thing to do. But what with this cold weather –

Anyway, so there I am out in this alleyway in

my pyjamas, the trilby warming my bald patch, when who should float out of the shadows but my old mate Alfie Spectre.

I've known Alfie since I was a small boy. He lives just down the road there, about a minute's float from this very hotel. At least, he did when he was still alive.

'Hello, Alfie,' I said, doffing my trilby. 'Fancy meeting you here.'

'Hello, Charlie,' Alfie said with a smirk.

The minute we'd decided to holler-day in Frighten, I'd called Alfie on the phantom phone, told him we should meet for a spot of business.

That's how I make my living, if you pardon the pun. I buy and sell whatever I can lay my haunted hands on.

'What have you got for me this cold winter's night?' I said.

Alfie unfastened his buttons and there they were, half a dozen gold watches pinned to the lining of his army coat.

'Are they hot, Alfie?' I said. That's a cockney way of asking if the watches were stolen.

Now, don't get me wrong, I'm no angel – that's a trilby on my head, not a halo – but I don't buy stolen goods. I'm a gentleman, see?

'Nothing's hot in this weather,' Alfie said with a wink.

'That's good enough for me,' I said, and I bought all six.

But something was wrong.

When Alfie counted those pound notes and tucked them into his pocket, his hands were trembling like he'd seen a, um, ghost.

Alfie had been a soldier, he'd been killed in the trenches, that's why I'm in my forties and poor Alfie is still only twenty-one. He was a brave lad, our Alfie, and it took a lot to make his hands shake.

'Alfie, whatever is the matter?'

'Do you have far to float home, Charlie?'

I glanced at the brickwork to my left, and gave Alfie a wink. 'A pass-through, a wisp and a float, and I'll be tucked up in no time.'

'I'd get going, if I were you,' Alfie said. 'There's a lot of funny people about.'

'How do you mean?'

Alfie lowered his voice. 'Charlie, there's been – shall we say, sightings.'

This made me laugh so hard I almost dropped my hat. 'That'll be my old mate Headless Leslie. He wisped down to Frighten for his summer holler-days and forgot the way home.'

Alfie frowned. It was hard to tell in the glow of the streetlamp, but his face looked white. 'I've met your mate Leslie, and this wasn't him. This chap was a good deal more sinister than your mate Leslie.'

'Rubbish,' I said, and I tried to do that thing where you flick the rim of your trilby with your finger and it does a somersault and you catch it on your elbow.

Trouble was, Alfie had got me nervous, and I poked out the wrong elbow and missed my target. The trilby tumbled into the darkness.

As I lifted the trilby from a frosty puddle I heard this muffled yell, and when I wisped back up Alfie had gone.

It ain't like Alfie to float off without saying goodbye. He's playing a prank on me, I told myself as I tightened the cord of my dressing gown. A regular joker, is our Alfie. He'll be hiding behind a wall, I thought, ready to wisp

out and yell BOO.

That was when this creepy feeling came over me, like I was being watched.

When I turned around, there it was. A figure dressed in black, a top hat on its head, two red eyes peering out from behind this flowing purple cape.

So now I knew why Alfie Spectre had wisped off.

I didn't stop to find out where he'd got to. I passed through that wall as quick as my transparent bits would float me, and wisped off to bed.

5
The Fortune Teller

'You look terrible,' Tabitha said when we gathered on the beach the following afternoon.

'Wither snores,' I said.

All right, so that weren't the real reason I hadn't slept. The truth is, after seeing that caped figure in the alleyway I'd spent the rest of the night staring into the darkness.

I kept thinking I should tell the other ghosties about what I'd seen, but I didn't want to spoil the holler-day.

Agatha floated down the sandy wooden steps that led up onto the pier. 'The pier is closed,' she said, fiddling with the brim of her floppy sunhat. 'Some holler-day this has turned out to be. I told you we should have gone to Scare-borough.'

'We can always find a way to amuse ourselves,' said Tabitha. 'Perhaps some of these amusement machines are switched on.'

'You could make them work,' said Pamela, 'using your poltergeist skills.'

'I'm afraid my poltergeist skills just aren't that powerful,' Tabitha said. 'I can make a policeman's helmet topple from his head, or a cyclist cycle backwards, but electricity is something else.'

'I want candyfloss,' Humphrey said, bumping into a brightly painted candyfloss machine.

'If Humphrey doesn't get his candyfloss,' Agatha said, 'we'll never hear the end of it.'

'Hide your eyes then,' said Tabitha. 'I'm awfully shy, you know.'

Me, Humphrey and Pamela covered our eyes with our hands, and Agatha hid behind her floppy sunhat.

It's not the polite thing to do, I know, but I couldn't help peeking. Well, I bet the other ghosties did the same.

The turny thing turned and the whizzy bit whizzed, and this big tuft of pink candyfloss oozed through a tube and into a plastic bag, which popped out through an opening in the bottom of the machine. Humphrey grabbed it with a greedy hand and licked his lips.

It was at that moment that I spotted this stripy tent thing on the edge of the beach. 'There is one attraction still open,' I said. 'Look.'

A wooden sign at the entrance read FORTUNE TELLER. We all wisped in through the open flap, and I paid the fortune teller 50p.

The old woman fixed me with her eerie gaze,

rubbed this crystal ball with her hands, and
started to spout drivel about our future.

'Ye shall find what ye seek on the pier,' the
old woman moaned, and when she nodded her
head her hoop earrings jiggled. 'Even though it
is closed for the duration,' she added. 'Seek, and
ye shall find.'

'She means Headless Leslie,' Agatha
whispered.

'And you, miss,' the fortune teller groaned,
staring into Agatha's eyes, 'will breeze about in
a floppy sunhat, and you, boy,' she wailed,
turning to Humphrey, 'will bump into things
and annoy the seagulls.'

'What a frightfully accurate reading,' Agatha
blushed.

'It's almost like she's one of us,' I said.

'Funny you should say that, Charlie,' Pamela
said, 'but the fortune teller looks like Wither.'

'I say,' said Tabitha, 'where is Wither?'

'And you will all stop being mean to Wither,'
the fortune teller went on, 'and you will allow
him to recite poetry all day, and—'

Tabitha laughed, and Humphrey bumped
into the table, and the crystal ball rolled onto
the floor, and the fortune teller tumbled from
her chair, the wig falling from her bald head.

'Wither!' Agatha said. 'Who'd have thought you'd look so delightful in a dress?'

Wither tore off the dress, revealing his ordinary clothing, folded his arms, and started to blub.

6
The Old
Victorian Pier

'That was a rotten stunt, Wither,' Pamela said as the six of us floated up the rickety wooden steps to the pier.

'Wither didn't mean any harm,' I said, though only to stop him blubbing. I even put my arm around the bony fool. 'He was just getting into the holler-day spirit, weren't you, Wither?'

'That's right,' said Wither, wiping his eyes. 'The holler-day spirit, like Charlie said.'

'Well, we thought you were highly entertaining,' said Tabitha. 'Didn't we, Humphrey?'

Humphrey nodded, and gave his candyfloss a lick.

'Never mind all that,' I said, straightening my trilby. 'Look.'

The pier's ornate iron gates were secured with a chain, fastened with a heavy padlock. A sign hung across the bars read: FRIGHTEN PIER CLOSED UNTIL SPRING.

'We'll never get this thing off,' Humphrey said, examining the heavy padlock. 'Not without a skeleton key.'

'How are we meant to find poor Leslie if we can't get onto the pier?' said Tabitha.

'Perhaps there's a key hung on a hook on the other side,' I said. The bars were too close together to poke your head between them, so I doffed my trilby – the polite thing to do – and passed through the metal. 'No,' I said, passing back. 'Not a dickybird.'

'The key may be hidden from prying eyes,' said Pamela, and she wisped over the top of the gate to have a look.

We floated about for a minute or so, watching the seagulls squawk and flap, and then Wither wrinkled his brow. 'I have to say, Pamela is taking her time.'

A horrible thought occurred to me at that point. What if my mate Alfie Spectre hadn't wisped off down that alleyway last night? What if he'd been nabbed by that figure in the cape and top hat? And what if that same haunted heinousity had captured our Pammy?

Poor Pamela Fraidy, I thought as I peered between the bars. She's a nervous wreck as it is, and that caped figure is enough to give any ghosty a fright.

'She was probably distracted by the

attractions,' Agatha said. 'You know how flitty she is.'

'Yes,' I said nervously. 'She's just having a look around, that's all.'

'Charlie,' Tabitha said, 'you're shaking. Whatever is the matter?'

'It's this cold weather,' I said. I passed through the gate for a quick flit, and when I saw Pamela I breathed a sigh of relief. 'There she is, by the slot machines. And look, she's found the key. Wither, Humphrey, wisp over the gate and tell Pamela to float back and let us in.'

Wither and Humphrey frowned and wisped off.

Two minutes passed, and the ghosties did not return.

'It's getting dark,' I said. 'We need that key, or we'll be floating about out here all night.'

'Float after them, Aggie,' said Tabitha, and

Agatha adjusted her floppy sunhat and floated off, leaving just Tabitha and myself.

Two minutes passed, and Agatha did not return.

'I can see Humphrey,' Tabitha said a minute later. 'He's eating an I-scream.'

'I could pass through the gate,' I said, 'round up the four of them, grab the key from Pamela and flit back.'

'No need,' said Tabitha, and over the gate she wisped.

7
Hall of Mirrors

I decided I'd better tell the other ghosties about the caped figure. If I didn't, and that top-hatted horror nabbed me like it had nabbed Alfie Spectre, the other ghosties would never know what had happened.

Tabitha is the most sensible ghosty, so I approached her the moment I'd floated over the gate. 'Tabitha, there is something I have to tell you.'

'You can tell me when we're all together,' Tabitha said. 'Where did the other ghosties wisp off to? Let's try in here.' And she wisped beneath the door of this long wooden hut.

Along the side of the hut the words HALL OF MIRRORS were painted in huge white letters. I doffed my hat at the sign – an odd thing to do, perhaps, but a polite thing to do all the same – and passed through the wood.

'There's Pamela,' Tabitha said.

'Where?' I said, glancing at my reflection in one of the mirrors. The wobbly glass made my head look like a grape with a pencil-thin moustache.

'There,' Tabitha said, pointing.

I turned to where Pamela Fraidy was cowering in a corner by one of the mirrors, chewing her fingernails and quivering.

'Poor Pammy,' Tabitha said. 'These mirrors can give one quite a fright, and Pamela Fraidy is a nervous wreck as it is.'

As Tabitha and myself wisped to the rescue, I caught sight of a top hat reflected in one of the mirrors.

'Then we must escort her to safety,' I said, doffing my trilby at the caped figure's reflection. 'After all, it is the polite thing to do.'

I grabbed Tabitha and Pamela by the hand and wisped them under the door.

8
Bumper Cars

'Pamela,' Tabitha said as we flitted about outside, 'I need to have a word with Charlie. Would you mind awfully?'

I thought perhaps Tabitha had seen the caped figure in the Hall of Mirrors.

'Not at all,' Pamela said, and she folded her arms and turned the other way. 'One knows when one is not wanted.'

'You are wanted, Pammy,' Tabitha said. 'I just need to have a word with Charlie, that's all.'

'About what?' Pamela said, peering at

Tabitha over her shoulder. 'Nothing to worry about, I hope?'

'Not at all,' said Tabitha. 'I say, isn't that Humphrey on the Bumper Cars?'

We floated over the planks, waves crashing far below, to a brightly painted arena with the words BUMPER CARS painted across the front.

'It looks frightfully fun,' Tabitha said.

'I'd say it looks frightfully frightening,' Pamela said.

We watched for a bit, then Pamela said, 'Shouldn't he be sat at the wheel, rather than bumping the cars with his belly?'

'He'll be sick,' Tabitha said, 'bumping about after all that candyfloss and I-scream.'

I floated into the red car and Humphrey squeezed in beside me, and Tabitha and Agatha wisped into a green car with a dented bonnet.

'The electricity is switched off,' I said.

'Humphrey, you will have to get out and bump.'

'Tabitha,' Humphrey said, 'you could boot up the electricity using your skills.'

'What skills?' said Tabitha, shyly.

A moment later, however, the light bulbs hung around the top of the arena illuminated the night sky, red and yellow and blue and green, and this waltzy-schmaltzy music started up and the cars began to move.

Bump, bump, bump!

9
Ghost Train

When we got off the Bumper Cars, Pamela had turned as white as a, um, ghost, and Humphrey looked like he was about to be sick.

'I never knew bumping could be such fun,' Tabitha said, and she bumped into me, Pamela and Humphrey.

'This is no time for japes,' I said. 'We have to find the other ghosties before—'

Before the caped figure nabs them, I thought to myself, but I didn't say this out loud. I didn't want to frighten poor Pamela.

'Talking of finding the other ghosties,' Tabitha said, 'isn't that dear old Withaniel?'

Withaniel is Wither's full first name. Withaniel Scunthorpe the Third.

'Where?' I said. I could just make out the blue-black line where the sea met the sky, with the rides and amusements silhouetted against the night.

'It's difficult to see much in the dark,' Tabitha said. And she winked at me, and another string of bulbs lit up, and then another and another, until every bulb on Frighten Pier glowed a garish hue.

We floated over to a spookily painted building with cut-outs of skeletons and spectres nailed to the front, the words GHOST TRAIN painted across the top in luminous yellow paint.

'Wither,' Tabitha said, 'what are you doing?'

Wither looked up from where he was sat in one of the cars. 'The ghosties keep being mean to me. I'm going home.'

'I'm sure they didn't mean it, Wither.'

'Don't go home,' I said, doffing my trilby.

'We're on holler-day.'

'I need a holler-day from your meanness,' Wither said, and the wheels began to turn and the row of cars rolled along the track and in through a spookily painted wooden door.

'Your doing?' I asked Tabitha.

A minute later, this other spookily painted door opened and the row of cars rumbled out and came to a halt.

Wither frowned. 'I seem to have missed my stop.'

'This train won't take you home,' Tabitha said. 'The Ghost Train is a fairground ride. It's meant to be scary.'

'But it isn't scary at all,' Wither said. 'There's just a handful of jingly-jangly skeletons and so forth.'

'That doesn't mean it will take you home,' said Tabitha, and again the train of cars disappeared into the tunnel.

10
Ferris Wheel

After two more goes on the Ghost Train, Wither admitted defeat and floated out from the car. 'The only place that train takes you is back where you started.'

'We did try to explain,' Tabitha said kindly.

'I say, what happened to the other ghosties?' Wither said, glancing round.

'We're trying to round them up,' I said.

Wither looked at me like I'd gone mad. 'We?'

'Me and Tabitha,' I said. 'We've found Pammy and Humphrey, and—' But when I turned around, Tabitha, Pamela and Humphrey had gone. 'Now where might those three have wisped off to?'

'I'm in here, with Humphrey,' I heard Tabitha call. 'Though I don't know what happened to Pamela.'

Wither and myself followed Tabitha's floaty, ghostly voice further up the pier to a covered arcade. Flickering lights spelt the word AMUSEMENTS across the front. Inside, the arcade was lined with slot machines, one-armed bandits, that sort of thing.

'We'd better find the others,' I told Tabitha. 'There is something sinister going on, and—'

'Not yet,' Tabitha said. 'Humphrey and I are about to make our first million.'

Tabitha and Humphrey were floating above a carpet of coins that glistened silver and gold in the glare of the garish bulbs.

'What the devil are you doing?' Wither asked.

'Cheating,' Humphrey said, and he gave one of the machines an almighty bump with that big greedy belly. Several hundred coins

clattered to the floor.

Wither pulled a face like he was chewing a wasp. 'This is dishonest.'

'We won't keep a penny of it,' Tabitha said. 'We just wanted to feel rich for a moment, that's all. Come on, Humphrey. We must find the others.'

'Money isn't everything,' Humphrey said with a glum shrug. He gave the coins a wave goodbye and followed Wither, Tabitha and myself out into the night.

Outside, we flitted about until I spotted Pamela and dear Aggie, screaming their haunted heads off at the top of the Ferris Wheel.

'Such high spirits,' Wither said as we looked up.

'Yes,' Tabitha said. 'They're enjoying themselves immensely.'

'We'll never find Leslie at this rate,' Wither said with a blub.

I was about to doff my trilby when I thought I saw something black circle against the night sky.

Tabitha fixed me with a serious gaze. 'Charlie, whatever is the matter? You've been on edge all afternoon.'

'Nothing,' I told her, and I straightened my tie.

'But there is something wrong, isn't there? You've seen something. I know because I've seen it too. A caped figure dressed in black.'

'You've seen it too?'

'What's all this about a caped figure?' Wither said.

I shrugged. 'Um, would you like to buy a wristwatch?'

11
The Old Victorian Music Hall

When we were all together, myself, Tabitha Tumbly, Wither, Humphrey Bump, Agatha Draft and a somewhat shaken Pamela Fraidy, we set off in search of Headless Leslie.

To Tabitha and myself, the matter had become urgent. We were the only two ghosties who knew about the caped figure in the top hat.

'We should split up, Charlie,' Wither said.

'Rubbish. It took us an hour to find each other.'

'Charlie is right,' Tabitha said. 'And I don't think any of us should be alone on a pier on a dark winter's evening.'

'There's a lot of funny people about,' I added, thinking back to when Alfie Spectre had used these exact words.

'Who knows what horrors may lurk,' Wither groaned.

'Shh,' Agatha said. 'You'll frighten Pamela.'

'What's all this talk of horrors?' Pamela asked Wither.

'It's nothing,' Tabitha told her, touching her quivering arm. 'Wither was reciting a poem. Weren't you, Wither?'

'If it's nothing,' Pamela said, 'why are you and Charlie so afraid? Tabitha, you and Charlie Vapour are the bravest ghosties I know. If this – this horror – is enough to unnerve the two of you, then it must be truly frightful.'

'Honest,' Tabitha said, 'it's nothing. Charlie and I have overactive imaginations.'

'Yes,' I said, straightening my trilby. 'The

mind plays tricks. Let's get on with our search.'

We flitted between the rides for a bit, but found no sign of Headless Leslie, not so much as a head.

'There is only one place left to look,' Wither said in his poetry voice. 'At the end of the pier, where the wind howls, the wood creaks and the seagulls fear to flap.'

Pamela wisped behind Tabitha and plugged her ears with her fingers.

'But where at the end of the pier?' Tabitha said.

Wither extended a bony finger, and pointed towards a rickety building with no windows and an angular wooden staircase leading up to a grand doorway. The sight of the wonky roof prompted me to straighten my trilby.

'Off you go then,' I told the cowardly old fool. 'We'll wait out here.'

'You won't catch me in there,' Wither said.

'What is that building anyway?'

'That,' Agatha said, 'is the Old Victorian Music Hall. It's a sort of musical theatre. There'll be rows of seats and a stage with a red velvet curtain.'

'Why didn't you say so?' said Wither. 'I love musical theatre.' And he floated off towards the building.

A moment later, he floated back.

'Wither,' Tabitha said, 'whatever is the matter?'

'I saw – a shadow.'

'There are a lot of shadows,' Agatha told Wither breezily. 'It's a dark winter's evening, and we're on a pier lit by fairground lights.'

No sooner had these words blown from Agatha's lips when the lights went out. Every bulb on that pier fizzed and crackled and popped, leaving us poor ghosties with only the moon to light our way.

'Perhaps someone flipped the lever,' Tabitha said.

'Either that or it flipped itself,' said Humphrey, and Pamela hid behind the curve of his belly.

'I felt a spot of rain,' Agatha said, arching an elegant hand. 'Let's float inside.'

'What's that sound?' Wither cried, clamping a bony hand to his mouth. 'I heard a sound like – like souls escaping from a morgue.'

'It's just the wind,' Tabitha said.

'All perfectly innocent then,' said Wither. 'Just one point, however. A moment ago there were six of us. And now, quite suddenly, there are seven.'

'Rubbish,' I said. 'You miscounted.'

'Then who is that chap in the purple cape,

with eyes like burning coals and a tombstone top hat?'

'Ghosties,' I said, as the caped figure towered overhead, 'I think we had better wisp off.'

12

Trapped!

As we floated up the rickety old stairs of the Old Victorian Music Hall, the door swung open, which somehow felt both welcoming and terrifying at the same time, and we found ourselves in this vast candlelit space.

The door slammed behind us with a THUD.

'Bump it,' I told Humphrey, and he bumped and bumped and bumped, but the door would not open.

'The wood is too heavy,' Humphrey said, his hair standing on end, 'and the bolt is orange with rust.'

'That door is the only thing around here that isn't falling apart,' said Pamela Fraidy.

'You speak for yourself,' said Wither.

We wisped this way and that, 'henceforth and sideways,' as Wither put it, the daft old goat, until Agatha Draft rattled her pearls and declared that we were trapped.

'Trapped?' Wither said, gripping his jaw with his quill-like fingers.

'Trapped,' Agatha said.

The six of us floated about for a bit, then Wither said, 'So we're trapped then?'

'Trapped,' Agatha said, and she clutched her pearls to her chest.

'Trapped, trapped, trapped!' Wither cried, his poetry voice echoing around the hall. I told him to stop blubbing, and he turned to me and said, 'It's all right for you, Charlie Vapour. You can pass through. The rest of us are trapped, trapped, trapped!'

'Wither is right,' Tabitha said. 'Charlie, you can float off home whenever you like.'

'And leave my ghostly friends in Frighten with that caped figure?'

'But what a place to be trapped,' said Agatha. 'Tabitha, light the rest of those candles.'

'Turn away then,' Tabitha said, and we turned away. When we turned back, the Old Victorian Music Hall was lit by the warm glow of the hundreds of candles that lined the walls.

'I say,' Pamela said. 'What a charming interior.'

'It's like an old-fashioned cinema,' Humphrey

said, 'but without the screen.'

Wither shook his head. 'It's more like a church, but with comfy seats instead of pews.'

To me it looked like exactly what it was. A shabby old musical theatre, the sort that makes you want to take your hat off.

'Spook-tacular it may be,' Pamela said, 'but we still need to find the way out.'

'Perhaps Leslie knows the way out,' Tabitha said. 'We must find him. And I know how.'

Wither arched an eyebrow. Then, he arched the other eyebrow. 'Oh yes?'

'This musical theatre is the reason Headless Leslie floated to Frighten in the first place. There is nothing Leslie likes more than musical theatre.'

'You think Leslie might be trapped in here with us?' Pamela said.

'If he's not inside, he'll be somewhere close by.'

'But how do we find him?' Agatha said.

'Look around you,' said Tabitha. 'We have curtains, a stage, and row upon row of seats.'

'Explain,' I said, politely doffing my hat.

'We put on a show,' Tabitha said, 'and wait for Leslie to come to us.'

'What a splendid idea,' Wither said.

'Every ghosty loves a show,' said Agatha.

13
Headless Leslie

I went on first.

I grabbed this elegant cane from backstage, tipped my trilby and performed a dapper tap dance. Tabitha did her best to follow me with the spotlight. My shoes passed through the wood, so I made the tapping sound with a click of the tongue.

By the time I'd finished my second number, every seat in the Old Victorian Music Hall was occupied. Ghosties had wafted in from all over Frighten. How the ghosties got into the building I don't know, but judging by how see-through they were, I reckon they were the sort who ain't got much presence, if you know what I mean.

Next up was Agatha Draft, who blew a terrifying tune on the Old Victorian Pipe Organ. The audience found Agatha's tune terribly moving, so moving in fact that the front two rows blew away.

Then came Pamela's turn. She'd promised us a tune, but no sooner had she sung the first note than she got stage fright. Tabitha had to lower the curtain while Agatha led her from the stage.

I was hoping that would be the end of the show, but Wither insisted on reciting one of his poems. Funnily enough, it all worked out for the best.

Most theatres have a trapdoor in the centre of the stage, and this theatre was no different. The moment Wither cleared his throat, Humphrey Bump did the decent thing and bumped the lever that operates the trapdoor, and the trapdoor dropped open.

Now, ghosties can't stand on floorboards, as you know, but the trapdoor created a draft, and the draft sucked old Shakespeare through the square hole, and he vanished into the darkness.

'Humphrey, there was no call for that,' Agatha said.

'Oh, I don't know,' I said. 'Wither's poems are frightful.'

'I have to admit, you have a point,' Agatha said. 'But even so.'

'We'd better find him,' said Tabitha, wisping out from behind the curtain.

'Wait,' Pamela said. 'Look who's turned up.'

'Headless Leslie,' Tabitha said, and we all floated down to the front row, where Leslie was sat with his head in his lap, his fingers plugging the ears.

'Wither's poems are drivel,' Leslie said.

'I don't think we'll be hearing any more from Wither for a while,' I said.

The trapdoor had swung shut, and I was the only ghosty who had noticed. I should have mentioned this to Tabitha, but, well, I had to say hello to my old mate Leslie, and what with one thing and another—

Let's just say I forgot.

14

The Magician

'It looks like there's another act,' Leslie said, lifting his head onto his shoulders. Leslie wears this Elizabethan ruffle collar, so the head stays on a treat. It only falls off when he nods it, which explains why Leslie never agrees to anything.

We were all sat in the front row, the girls to Leslie's left, Humphrey and me to his right. Tabitha had closed the red velvet curtain, but now it began to twitch and sway, and as the curtain lifted, the spotlight settled on the bare wooden boards of the stage.

'There's no need for that,' I told Tabitha. 'We've all performed our party pieces, and

Leslie's turned up.'

'Most of the audience have faded away,' Humphrey said, glancing behind at the rows and rows of empty seats. 'Let's find the way out and float off home.'

'It wasn't me,' Tabitha said.

I gulped. 'If it wasn't you, then who—'

Pamela hid under her seat.

Then the organ started up, sort of whirly and swirly, and who should waft garlic-like onto the stage but the caped figure.

If I'd still had skin, I'd have leapt out of it.

'It's all right, Charlie,' Agatha said, clutching her pearls. 'He's a magician, and he's here to perform his breathtaking illusions. I read about him in a leaflet back at the hotel.'

'That explains the mantelpiece moustache and candlestick sideburns,' said Pamela, floating out from beneath her seat.

'But that's the ghosty who nabbed my mate

Alfie Spectre.'

'Agatha is right,' Tabitha said. 'That ghosty is an authentic Victorian conjuror. His name is The Great Conjuro.'

'What a splendid name,' I said, still shaken, I have to admit.

'If there is anything sinister going on,' Agatha said, 'we'll find out soon enough. Until then, I intend to sit back and enjoy the performance.'

So that was that. Nabbed mate or no nabbed mate, there was nothing for it but to settle in our velvet seats and watch the show.

And what a show it was!

First, he pulled this silk hanky from his pocket and stuffed it into his left hand, and when he opened his hand the hanky had vanished. He then pulled the hanky out of his sock and blew his nose.

Then, he produced an umbrella from behind

his elbow, and the umbrella turned into a bouquet of flowers and the flowers turned into a sword and the sword turned into a deck of playing cards and the cards turned into a bowl of smiling goldfish.

You should have heard our applause when The Great Conjuro vanished the bowl up his sleeve!

'For my grand finale,' the magician said in his booming cannonball voice, 'I will perform the greatest illusion in all magic.'

Agatha gasped.

'For this trick I require a volunteer from the audience,' The Great Conjuro said. Then he coughed into the back of his hand and added, 'One who doesn't mind having his head sawn off.'

'I volunteer,' Agatha said, raising a swan-like hand.

'I have to say,' Pamela said, 'you're terribly brave. I would volunteer myself, but the truth is, I'm afraid.'

'Pick me, pick me!' Agatha shrieked, but the magician grabbed Headless Leslie by the arm and wisped him onto the stage.

'That's not fair,' Agatha wept. 'Leslie didn't even volunteer.'

'I wonder why he chose Headless Leslie,'

I said, and the other ghosties shrugged.

'Perhaps Leslie's tunic looks good under the stage lights,' Pamela said.

The magician floated behind the curtain stage-left, then floated back, wheeling an ornate wooden box.

'Why does the box have eight wheels,' I said. 'Four would be enough, surely.'

'The box has eight wheels,' Agatha said, 'so that the magician can separate the box into two sections at the end of the trick. My father took me to magic shows all the time, when I was a little girl.'

'I don't know why he has to saw Leslie's head off,' Pamela said. 'Why not just shake him by the hand and bid him good day?'

'Shh,' said Agatha. 'The greatest illusion in all magic is about to begin.'

15

The Magician's Illusion

The moment Leslie lay back in the ornate wooden box, The Great Conjuro closed the lid.

With a flourish of his cape, the magician produced a saw from thin air, and the organ music stopped and this ghostly orchestra materialised in the orchestra pit. The magician sawed a notch in the wooden box, about a head's length from the end, and began to saw through the wood.

'I genuinely do not know how this trick is done,' said Agatha Draft.

'It's simple,' said Tabitha. 'You see—'

Agatha covered her ears with her hands. 'Don't tell me.'

'Leslie's head is detachable, as you know, and—'

'I don't want to hear this,' Agatha said.

The magician sawed and sawed and sawed, until the wooden box broke into two sections. We all gasped, then clapped our haunted hands.

'Incredible,' I said.

'Breathtaking,' said Tabitha Tumbly.

'Horrific,' cried Pamela Fraidy.

'Awesome,' grinned Humphrey Bump.

'I wish he'd saw Wither's head off,' Agatha said. 'I say, where is Wither?'

'He's still down that trapdoor,' I said. 'I suppose we'd better rescue him. If he has to find his own way out, we'll never hear the end of it.'

'I'm not going down there,' Pamela said. 'It's dark, and there'll be plankton.'

'I don't think any of us want to go down

there,' Agatha said. 'That's why it was so terribly mean of Humphrey to bump that lever.'

'Wither will be all right,' said Tabitha. 'He'll find a knot in the wood and wisp out into the night.'

'Shh,' Agatha said. 'We're missing the show.'

The Great Conjuro took a bow, then wheeled the head-sized end of the ornate wooden box away from the main section, and lifted it from the metal frame so that we could see Leslie's smiling head inside.

As the five of us floated up from our seats to applaud, the magician bowed so low that the head-end of the box tipped up and Leslie's head rolled out. The ghostly head did not stop rolling until it dropped through a gap in the boards at the back of the stage.

'The magician did that on purpose,' I said. 'I knew something was up, and this proves it.'

'Nonsense,' Agatha said.

The Great Conjuro bowed once more, and vanished in a puff of purple smoke.

Agatha frowned. 'Oh dear.'

'He's probably gone to fetch the head,' said Tabitha.

I removed my hat and scratched my bald patch. 'He's a magician, Tabitha. If he wanted the head back he'd conjure it up with his magic.'

'It isn't real magic,' Tabitha said.

'Oh, I'm quite sure it is real,' Agatha said breezily. 'At least, I like to think so.'

'It's all done with misdirection and sleight of hand,' Tabitha explained.

'And mirrors,' Pamela said. 'And lengths of cable with trumpets on the end.'

'I have to say,' Tabitha said, glancing down at her knees, 'I think Charlie might be right. Whether the magician uses real magic or skills, or, um, dangling trumpets, it's difficult to imagine such a talented ghosty dropping a head by mistake.'

'That's exactly what I thought,' I said, straightening my trilby.

'And if he had gone to fetch the head,' Tabitha said, 'wouldn't he be back by now?'

16
Velvet Trousers

Wither could find his own way out, but unless we rescued Leslie's head, it would spend several years rolling around in the dust – sneezing, due to Leslie's dust allergy – while the rest of him wandered in circles.

'It won't budge,' said Humphrey Bump. He was trying to shift the lever so that we could float down the trapdoor, but he kept bouncing off.

Us ghosties can wisp through a hole the size of a moth's nostril, and I can pass through, but it's preferable to have a bit of elbow room, if you know what I mean, and for breakfast that morning Humphrey had eaten twelve plates of chips.

Not only that, but the trapdoor would have let in some light.

'The magician must have jammed the lever,' Agatha said, 'using magic.'

'Or sleight of hand,' said Tabitha.

'There's nothing else for it,' Pamela said with a gulp. 'We will have to wisp into the darkness.'

'Let's not be hasty,' Tabitha said. 'There has to be another way down.'

'Tabitha,' I said after a quick nose around, 'I've found a door, and a staircase leading downwards.'

The trapdoor was situated in the centre of the stage, like I said, but the door was at the back, tucked away behind the curtain. I'd found the door by doffing my hat and passing through the curtain, and I knew there was a staircase behind the door because I'd passed through the wood.

'We could wisp under the door,' Pamela said, 'but that would be no better than wisping through a gap in the floorboards. Tabitha, you must use your skills.'

'All right,' Tabitha said, 'but do allow me a little privacy. You know how shy I am.'

Agatha, Pamela, Humphrey and myself faced the other way, and we heard this curtain-woosh sound and a clicky-clicky turning sound, and when we looked back, the curtain had been drawn to the side and the door swung on its hinges.

'Bravo, bravo,' Agatha said, clapping her ivory hands.

'Really,' Tabitha said, 'it was nothing.'

'I doubt this will take us below the stage,' Pamela said. 'The stairs lead off to the side.'

'It's worth a try,' said Tabitha. 'Show us the way, Charlie.'

'Um, ladies first,' I said, hiding behind my trilby.

'After you, Charlie Vapour,' Agatha said.

'I suppose it's up to me,' said Tabitha Tumbly, but just as she was about to wisp off, my hat toppled from my head and sailed down the staircase.

'Tabitha, you did that with your powers, so I'd have to float down and fetch it.'

'With my limited skills?' Tabitha said with a smile.

'You'd better fetch your hat,' Pamela said, 'before the magician nabs it.'

I adjusted my cufflinks and floated down into the darkness.

Then, I floated back up. 'My bald patch is cold,' I said, and Humphrey laughed.

'Get on with it,' Agatha said.

'Perhaps,' Pamela said, 'we should all float down together. It's less frightening that way.'

So the four of us joined hands and floated through the doorway and down the staircase, myself, then Tabitha, Pamela and Agatha, with Humphrey Bump bumping along at the rear, to the carpeted hallway at the bottom.

'It's not creepy at all,' said Pamela. 'Well, perhaps a little.'

The hallway was lined with seven doors, and one of the doors had been painted with a gold star.

'They're dressing rooms,' said Agatha. 'These are the rooms where the Victorian performers would rehearse their lines, apply make-up and prepare to tread the boards.'

'The room with the gold star will be the star's dressing room,' Tabitha said. 'Every show has a star, and the star would demand the grandest dressing room of all.'

'Then this,' I said, straightening my tie, 'is where we will find the magician.'

The moment I mouthed that final word, the door with the gold star creaked open, and an eerie purple light illuminated the dim hallway.

'Purple is The Great Conjuro's favourite colour,' said Agatha. 'I read that in a magazine.'

'Is he in there?' Pamela said, cowering behind Humphrey.

'I can't see anything with that purple light,' I said, but as I floated towards the dressing room door the light faded, and the interior of the dressing room wafted into view.

And there he sat, the mean-spirited magician in the purple cape and the black top hat.

'He's seen us,' I said, floating backwards. 'Perhaps we should wisp off.'

'But what about Leslie's head?' said Agatha. 'I say, where is Leslie?'

'The last time I saw him,' Pamela said, 'he was caught up in the stage curtain. I thought it best to leave him where he was.'

We all floated forwards and peered into the room. The Great Conjuro was sat on a chair, staring at his reflection in a mirror framed with bone-white light bulbs.

'I say,' Pamela said, 'the magician is awfully tall, even when seated.'

'I bet he's sitting on a plump cushion with tassels,' Agatha said. 'The Great Conjuro has frightfully good taste.'

'One way to find out,' I said. 'Agatha, waft the magician's cape with a ghostly draft.'

Agatha sighed. 'If only I had the required skill set.'

'This is no time for false modesty,' Tabitha said. 'The magician is sitting on something, and I think I can guess what it is.'

'Avert your gaze, then,' Agatha said.

We all closed our eyes – or pretended to – while Agatha rustled up an eerie breeze, and the magician's cape floated to one side and came to rest hooked over the back of the chair.

The Great Conjuro was not sat on a plump cushion with tassels as Agatha had thought. Wedged between the seat of the magician's velvet trousers and the chair was Leslie's head.

'Leslie!' I called in a loud whisper. 'Are you all right?'

'A tad squished,' Leslie said. 'Perhaps you could rescue me?'

Just as I was about to reply, The Great Conjuro fixed me with a magical gaze, tugging at the curve of his handlebar moustache.

We all floated back in horror, and tumbled about in the hallway.

'What a frightful predicament,' Agatha said. 'Poor Leslie.'

'I hope the magician is wearing clean underpants,' said Humphrey Bump.

17

Alfie Spectre

We were about to float back into the room when a door opened at the far end of the corridor. And who do you think floated out? None other than my old mate Alfie Spectre.

'Alfie! I thought you'd been nabbed.'

'I heard you had a spot of bother with The Great Conjuro,' Alfie said with a grin, 'so I floated over to see if I can help you out.'

I explained to Alfie that the magician had nabbed Leslie's head.

'The other week,' Alfie said, 'The Great Conjuro nabbed my mum's ghostly kitten.'

'What happened to the dear little thing?' Agatha asked, clutching her pearls.

'I gave the magician a gold ring, and he handed the kitten back unharmed.'

'Alfie buys and sells jewellery,' I explained. 'Watches, rings, that sort of thing.'

Tabitha coughed into the back of her hand. 'Where are your manners, Charlie?'

'Oh, right,' I said, straightening my tie. 'Alfie, these are my ghostly friends, Tabitha, Agatha, Pamela and Humphrey.'

'Charlie,' Tabitha said, 'perhaps you could give the magician a ring in exchange for Leslie's head.'

'That's the spirit,' Agatha said. 'There's always an answer if you put your heads together. No pun intended.'

'A ghostly head would cost you a lot more than a ring,' Alfie said. 'Unless the ring was highly valuable, of course.'

'I doubt we possess anything of high value,' Agatha said. 'Well, only my pearls—'

'And these,' I said, and I opened my jacket so the ghosties could see the half-dozen gold watches pinned to the lining. 'I bought these watches from Alfie during the night.'

Alfie scratched his head in thought. 'Charlie,' he said, 'those watches are exactly the sort of thing the magician would swap for a ghostly head.'

'How do you know so much about The Great Conjuro?' Humphrey asked, giving the boy a friendly bump.

'Oh, um. I must have read it somewhere.'

'Never mind that,' Leslie's head called out from the magician's dressing room. 'Just give the magician the watches and take me back to my body.'

To my relief, the moment I floated into the dressing room with my jacket open, The Great Conjuro smiled a twinkly, enigmatic smile and held out a white-gloved hand. I gave him the watches and flitted off.

'Charlie,' Tabitha said when I reached the doorway, 'I think you may have forgotten something.'

'You're right,' I said. 'It's nerves, see.'

Agatha rustled up a friendly breeze and blew me back into the dressing room.

'Erm, excuse me,' I said, holding my hat to my chest, 'I am sorry to trouble you, but I wonder if you will allow me the courtesy of – what I mean to say is – would you mind awfully—'

'Yes?' the magician boomed.

'Can we have our head back?'

'Certainly,' he replied, and immediately vanished in a puff of purple smoke.

So that was that. The Great Conjuro had wafted off, leaving us frightfully friendly ghosties to return the head to its rightful owner.

It wasn't until we floated up the stairs and

untangled poor Leslie from the curtains at the back of the stage, that we remembered poor Withaniel.

'We could have given the magician Wither's pocket watch,' Agatha said, holding the head in her elegant hands. 'That antique timepiece of his must be worth more than those six gold watches put together.'

'I say,' Agatha said, 'where is Wither?'

'He must still be down the trapdoor,' said Pamela.

Then we heard a muffled voice that seemed to come from the pocket of Alfie's army jacket. 'I never knew you were a ventriloquist, Alfie,' I said.

But Alfie looked as surprised as us lot.

'That sounded like Wither's voice,' Tabitha said. 'Alfie, I think you'd better unbutton your pocket.'

As Alfie unfastened the button, the flap flapped open and out wisped a certain Victorian poet.

'Wither,' Tabitha said, 'what were you doing in the pocket of Alfie's army jacket?'

'I didn't know it was Alfie's when I wisped into the pocket,' Wither said. 'The jacket was hung on a hook in one of the dressing rooms. I flitted into the pocket to hide from the magician.'

'Alfie likes to make himself at home,' I said with a wink. 'Ain't that right, Alfie?'

But Alfie just gazed down at his shoes.

'Alfred,' Wither said, 'it is time you returned Charlie's six gold watches.'

'I don't know what you're talking about,'

Alfie said, blushing a ghostly whitish red.

'You, Alfred,' Wither said, folding his bony arms, 'are a cheeky, lying rascal.' He pointed a wobbly finger at Alfie. 'This young man is in business with the magician. The Great Conjuro is nothing more than a great con artist.'

'Surely not,' Agatha gasped.

'Not only that, but Alfie here is his accomplice.'

Alfie held up his hands, protesting his innocence, but then he floated backwards and tripped over a heavy object caught up in the curtains. Tabitha parted the curtains using her skills, revealing an ornate wooden chest.

'Whatever is in that chest,' Alfie said, 'I don't know nothing about it.'

'Rubbish,' Wither said. 'I may be going deaf in my old age, but I could hear every word from that pocket.'

'What did you hear?' Tabitha asked him.

'Conversations between Alfred and the magician. It seems that the pesky pair have been working this scam for months.'

'And how does this scam work, Wither?'

'Well—'

'Wither,' I said, 'I think we should hear this from Alfie.'

'All right,' Alfie said. 'I'll come clean.'

And we gathered round and listened to what Alfie Spectre had to say.

'I sell the victim an item of value. Then, The Great Conjuro kidnaps a friend of theirs, and I tell the victim that the only way to save their friend is to offer the magician something of value in exchange.'

'And the victim gives the magician whatever it was you sold them,' Tabitha said.

Alfie grinned. 'I get to keep the goods and the victim's money.'

'That sounds like a lot of work,' I said. 'Most

criminals simply pick the victim's pockets, or break into their home and steal their ghostly television.'

'I'd end up in prison for that,' Alfie said. 'With this scam, the police would think I've done nothing wrong. It's the magician who does the nabbing, and no ghostly police force can arrest a magician.'

'The moment The Great Conjuro hears the jangle of handcuffs,' Agatha cried, clapping her hands, 'he will vanish in a puff of purple smoke!'

'Alfie,' Pamela said, 'what you and the magician have done is wrong. You didn't just steal Charlie's money. You stole our ghostly holler-day.'

'I was worried about you, Alfie,' I said. 'I really thought you'd been nabbed.'

'One further question,' Tabitha said to Alfie Spectre. 'You've told us what you get out of this

con trick. But what's in it for The Great
Conjuro?'

'I guess he just likes nabbing people,' Alfie
said, and he wisped off.

'You should flit after him,' Humphrey said.

'He'll be on the other side of the pier by now,'
I said, tidying my trilby. 'Alfie can out-wisp the
best of them.'

'Thanks awfully,' Leslie's head said as
Agatha returned it to Leslie's shoulders.

'Let's find the way out,' I said, 'and float off
home.'

'Aren't we forgetting something?' Wither said.
He floated towards the chest, flexed his bony
fingers and opened the ornate wooden lid.

The chest was filled to the brim with watches,
necklaces, bracelets and rings.

'We must return these items to their rightful
owners,' Tabitha said.

'You will do no such thing,' a cannonball

voice boomed, and we all flitted round.

There, floating above the orchestra pit, was that great con artist The Great Conjuro, with Alfie Spectre tucked beneath one arm.

'We thought we'd seen the last of you, Alfie,' I said.

'Me and Cedric have had a chat,' Alfie said.

'Cedric is my real name,' the magician explained. 'The Great Conjuro is a stage name.'

'We'd never have guessed,' smirked Humphrey Bump.

'The boy Alfie has made me see sense,' Cedric said. 'What Alfred and I have done is wrong, and, much as I enjoy the odd nab, we intend to mend our ways and return the valuable items to their owners.'

'We'd like to help,' Agatha said, and she fluttered her elegant eyelashes. 'That is, if you wouldn't mind.'

'Don't worry,' Alfie said, 'we're not going to

wisp off and keep the items for ourselves.'

'Oh, we do believe you,' Tabitha said, 'but we really would like to help, wouldn't we, ghosties?'

'How frightfully friendly,' the magician said, and he beamed a magnificent smile.

School of Meanies

Contents

1
Ghost School

Ghost School is boring. You get told off for bumping!

Bumping is my best thing. The only thing I like better than bumping is cake and lollipops, and the only thing I like better than cake and lollipops is bumping a box of cake and lollipops, and—

'Humphrey!'

It was Tabitha Tumbly. Tabitha is the youngest grown-up ghosty and the nicest of the lot – no fibbing!

'Humphrey Bump, what happened to that box of cake and lollipops?'

'The cat bumped it,' I said. 'I mean, the cat knocked it over, with her paws.'

Tabitha folded her arms and frowned at the upside-down cardboard box, and the lollipops scattered across the kitchen tiles and the splodged cake.

'Humphrey, are you fibbing?'

'No,' I said. 'I mean, yes. I mean, I don't know.'

We were in the kitchen at the back of the house, just me and Tabitha, and it was a school day but I didn't want to go.

'Put your blazer on,' Tabitha said. 'I'll float you to school.'

I looked at where I'd left my blazer in a heap on the kitchen table. 'I'm not going to school today.'

'But it's your first day back.'

'That's why I'm not going. The first day back is horrible.'

My blazer floated off the table and hovered behind me like a bat. Tabitha is a poltergeist. She can move things with her powers. No fibbing!

'Why don't you like the first day?' Tabitha asked as I poked my arms into the blazer.

'It's horrible. You haven't seen the other children all summer, and then you have to see them – and they make fun of you because you're fat!'

'Children can be so mean,' Wither said, floating in from the garden. 'And, Humphrey, you're not fat. You're just, er, overly proportioned.'

Wither is a poet. That's why nothing he says makes any sense.

'Come along, Humphrey,' Tabitha said, floating into the hall. 'We'd better wisp, or you'll be late.'

'I'll wisp with you,' said Wither. 'It's a lovely day for a wisp, and I need to stretch my transparent bits.'

Ghost School used to be a still-alive school, in the old days, but then it got run down, so the still-alives built a new school on the other side of the village.

'Wait,' I said as Ghost School loomed into view. 'I have to tie my shoelaces.' And I wisped behind an old oak tree and hid.

'Humphrey?' Tabitha said, floating back and forth. 'Humphrey, where did you go?'

'There's nobody here,' I said in a sort of tree voice. 'Just us trees, and—'

The two grown-up ghosties peered around the trunk, and Tabitha took my hand and led me back to the path.

'You'll be fine when you get there and see your friends waiting for you,' Wither said.

'I haven't got any friends,' I said. 'Everyone hates me.'

But then I spotted Samuel Spook and Phil and Fay Phantom flitting across the playground, and I let go of Tabitha's hand and bounced off through the school gates.

2

Haunted Homework

'Ghost School is stupid and rubbish, and, um, I'm not going to Ghost School ever again!'

I'd practised saying that all the way home, but then I saw Tabitha and Agatha chopping vegetables in the kitchen, and the words bounced about inside my head, and when I opened my mouth nothing came out.

'Humphrey, how was your first day back at Ghost School?' Tabitha asked as carrots rolled across the chopping board.

'It was, um, fun,' I said, bobbing by the
stove.

'Dinner will be ready soon,' Tabitha said.
'Pie, with your favourite side helping of
sausages, pie, sausage pie, chips, pie and
pizza.'

'Us girls are having salad,' Agatha said,
biting a pointy, pointless carrot.

'I'm not hungry,' I said, even though my
tummy felt like a cave.

'That's not like you,' Pamela said, emerging
from the larder, her arms piled up with plates.
Pamela Fraidy is always nervous, so the plates
rattled and clanged.

'Humphrey,' Agatha said as I floated out to
the hall, 'you look as if you've found a lollipop
and dropped it.'

On the stairs I floated past Wither and
Charlie Vapour. Charlie winked at me and took
off his hat.

'Master Bump,' Wither said, 'Charlie doffed his trilby, and you didn't so much as bid him good day.'

'I did the polite thing to do,' Charlie said. 'The least you can do, Humphrey, is do the polite thing to do too.'

'But it isn't a good day,' I said, bumping the banister. 'It's a rotten day, with knobs on.'

'Don't be mean,' said Wither, pursing his lips.

'Humphrey is sulking,' Charlie said. 'Today was the first day back at school. He'll feel right as rain tomorrow.'

At the top of the stairs I bumped through the bedroom door, then bumped it closed behind me. I had my own bedroom now that the still-alives had moved out. The grown-up ghosties shared the four-poster bed in their old room.

I rummaged through my blazer pockets

and pulled out a fluffy
doughnut. I was
halfway through
munching it when
I heard Charlie
and Tabitha
talking on the
landing.

'I don't know
what's got into
him,' Tabitha
was saying.
'He used to love
Ghost School. Have
a word with him,
Charlie.'

'You talk to him,
Tabitha. You're closer to him in age. Humphrey
won't listen to an old duffer like me.'

'But you're a man, Charlie. All boys

together! And you can pass through. In you float!'

Charlie Vapour can pass through doors and walls and, well, anything – even when he's got his hat on. I'm not telling fibs!

I'd just taken another bite of the doughnut when Charlie's head passed through the bedroom door.

Charlie winked at me and doffed his hat. 'Are you alright, son?' he said in his cockney accent.

I nodded. I had my mouth full.

'Glad to hear it,' Charlie said, and he passed back.

The door handle turned by itself – Tabitha using her powers again – and Tabitha floated into the room.

'Humphrey, I've brought you a snack,' Tabitha said, and she dropped a crusty pork pie onto the bed.

'That wouldn't feed a mouse.'

Tabitha smiled, sort of kind but telling me off at the same time. 'If you want your dinner, you will have to float to the kitchen.'

'I'm not hungry,' I fibbed.

'Then there really is something wrong. Either you're coming down with flu, or something happened at school and you're afraid to say what.'

'Nothing happened at school,' I said. 'I'm just doing my homework, that's all.'

'If that's true, the homework must be haunted and see-through,' Tabitha said, 'because all I can see are doughnut crumbs and a grumpy face.'

I looked up at Tabitha's big eyes and said, 'Tabitha, if I tell you something, do you promise not to be cross?'

Tabitha sat beside me on the bed. Well,

floated. Ghosties can't sit on things, they can only float above things.

'I got expelled,' I told her. 'I've been thrown out of Ghost School. For good.'

3
The Ghost Headmaster

After breakfast next morning, Tabitha Tumbly and Charlie Vapour wisped me straight to the Ghost Headmaster's office.

Charlie knocked on the door with his knuckles, doffed his hat – the polite thing to do, no fibbing! – and passed through the wood.

'Let's leave Charlie to it,' I said, and I tried

to wisp out of the window but Tabitha snapped
her fingers and the window slammed
shut.

The door to the Ghost Headmaster's office
opened, and Charlie was there in the doorway.
He looked like he'd seen a ghost.

'Best manners,' Charlie whispered into my
ear as Tabitha and me floated into the office.
'The Headmaster is in a bad mood.'

'He's always in a bad mood,' I said.

The Ghost Headmaster floated by the
window with his back to us. He wore his flowing
black cape and that hat like a black sandwich
with a bit of lettuce hanging off it.

'Close the door,' the Ghost Headmaster said in his vaporous voice, and the door slammed closed and Tabitha looked at me and winked. 'Right,' the Ghost Headmaster said, wisping round, 'what's all this about?'

'Um,' Charlie said, hiding behind his hat.

'Humphrey is a pupil here at Ghost School,' Tabitha said. 'At least, he was.'

'Ah, the Rotund Rascal,' the Ghost Headmaster said with a smiling moustache. 'That's what the teachers call the boy. Humphrey Bump, the Rotund Rascal.'

'I'm not a rascal,' I said, my voice shaking. 'I just bump a lot, for fun.'

'Yes,' the Ghost Headmaster said. 'And, thus, expulsion.'

Charlie frowned. 'If only Wither were here,' he whispered. 'Wither understands all that poetic talk.'

'What the Ghost Headmaster is saying,'

Tabitha whispered, 'is that the reason poor little Humphrey got expelled is because he bumps.'

'Always bounding about,' the Ghost Headmaster said as he sat in a transparent ghostly chair. 'The boy simply does not fit in. Humphrey Bump is a round peg in a square hole.'

'It's hardly my fault the hole is the wrong shape!' I yelled, and Charlie elbowed me in the tummy and told me to shush.

'Take, for instance, the brass-band incident,' the Ghost Headmaster went on. 'I'd arranged for a marching band to parade by the school gates. All went well, until Humphrey here bumped the conductor, and the conductor got his head stuck in the tuba and tumbled into the percussion section, and bounced off the big bass drum, and ended up up-ended in a hedge.'

'Bumping is fun,' I said, and I bumped
the Ghost Headmaster, knocking him off his
ghostly chair.

'You oaf!' the Ghost Headmaster cried,
wisping to his phantom feet. 'Get that boy out
of my school at once.'

4
Plums

That afternoon, I heard the clack-clack-clack
of the clicky-clacky typewriter, so I peered into
the study, and there was Wither typing up his
poems, and Agatha dialling a number on the
telephone, and Pamela, Charlie and Tabitha
floating by the window.

'Wither,' Charlie said, 'leave it to Agatha. By
the time the post-phantom delivers the letter
to the other ghost school and the ghostly head

teacher types a reply, Humphrey will be old enough for university.'

Wither wasn't typing up his poems as I'd thought. He was typing a letter to another ghost school!

'Don't be mean,' Wither said as he typed with one bony finger. 'The typewritten word carries a certain—'

'Let Wither waste his time if he likes,' Tabitha

said. 'Agatha, have you finished dialling that number yet?'

'My hair keeps blowing into my eyes,' Agatha said, 'and I dial a wrong digit and have to start all over again.'

Agatha Draught is the sort of ghosty who blows an eerie breeze wherever she floats. She's also dead posh.

'There!' Agatha said as she finally finished
dialling.

'Put this in your mouth,' Pamela said, and
she popped a purple plum between Agatha's lips.

'What is it?' Agatha said, sounding posher
than ever.

'A plum,' Pamela said, 'to make your voice
plummy.'

'Agatha's voice is plummy enough as it is,' Charlie said, adjusting his tie.

Tabitha and the other grown-up ghosties gathered round to listen as Agatha talked into the mouthpiece. 'We were wondering if you had room for our boy. Humphrey is the name. Humphrey Bump.' Agatha raised an eyebrow at this point, and plonked the telephone receiver back into its cradle.

'What happened?' Tabitha asked.

'The rotter hung up on me,' Agatha said.

Agatha telephoned several other ghost schools, but whenever she mentioned my last name, they hung up.

When Tabitha announced that there were no ghost schools left to call, I bounced through the door and bumped every ghosty in that study – no fibbing!

'Calm down, Humphrey,' Charlie said, straightening his trilby.

'Hooray!' I yelled. 'I won't have to go to Ghost School ever again.'

'I'm afraid Humphrey is right,' Tabitha said. Just as I was about to bounce off to the garden and bump the ghostly gardener into a prickly hedge, Tabitha added, 'There is only one thing for it. Humphrey will have to go to Still-Alive School, with the still-alive children.'

Wither tugged the smudged letter from the clicky-clacky typewriter and crumpled it into a ball. 'But, Agatha, the still-alive children are meanies.'

'It's a mean world,' Agatha said, plucking the plum from between her lips. 'And it's even meaner to those who do not possess a proper education.'

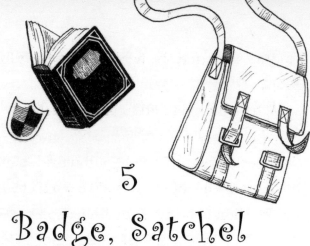

5

Badge, Satchel and Books

I spent the next few days stuffing my mouth with pies, sausages, pizza, pies and cake. If I make myself fat, I thought, my uniform won't fit and I won't have to go to Still-Alive School.

'Almost done,' Agatha said early on Monday morning. Me and the grown-up ghosties were floating about in the lounge, watching her sew a new badge onto my ghostly blazer. 'There,'

Agatha said, and she held up the blazer for all to see.

'Where did you find a ghost Still-Alive School badge?' I asked her, licking my lollipop.

'It's rather a sad tale,' Agatha said, almost in a whisper. 'One of the still-alive pupils climbed into the lion cage at the zoo. The lion ate him in one gulp. When he turned into a ghost, Charlie pinched the ghostly badge from his ghostly blazer.'

'I didn't pinch it,' Charlie said. 'I swapped it for a tub of raspberry-ripple I-scream.'

'Fancy being eaten by a lion,' said Pamela Fraidy. 'The very thought gives me the shivers.'

'Serves the boy right,' Wither said. 'This boy had a nasty habit of bopping felines on the head with a rolled-up comic. Kittens to begin with, then tabby cats and alley cats—'

'I guess he got greedy,' Agatha said. 'Now, try this on.'

'Thank you, Aunty Aggie,' I said. 'I can't wait to start my new school,' I added with a crafty smile.

I slipped my arms into the sleeves, then pulled the blazer at the front, but the buttons wouldn't reach the buttonholes, not even nearly.

'Humphrey,' Charlie said, wisping out from the lampshade, 'you've put on weight.'

'What a pity,' I said, tugging the blazer from my arms. 'I'll just have to stay at home and read comics.'

'You will do no such thing,' Agatha said.

'This explains why he's been eating so much,' Tabitha said.

'Humphrey, you should be ashamed of yourself.'

'You will have to go to Still-Alive School whether the blazer fits or not,' Agatha said.

'But the still-alive children will laugh at me,' I blubbed. 'They'll call me Small-Blazer and poke me with a stick.'

After breakfast, I found Wither and Tabitha in the hall.

'Humphrey,' Tabitha said, 'are you sure you don't want one of us to float to school with you?'

'No, it's fine,' I said as I tied my tie. 'I know the way.'

'Here's your satchel,' Wither said, passing me the horrible leather bag. 'I've packed the complete works of Shakespeare, Wordsworth and Dickens. Oh, I also included a few of my own writings, typed in double spacing on the clicky-clacky typewriter.'

'He'll never read all that,' Tabitha said.

She opened the front door using her poltergeist powers, and I floated out into the late-summer sun.

The moment Tabitha closed the door, I floated behind the hedge, dragging the phantom satchel. A second later, the door opened with an eerie creak.

'Can you see him?' I heard Tabitha ask.

'No, I can't,' Wither replied. 'He's so excited to meet his new friends, he'll be bouncing up that road without a care in the world.'

'I doubt he'll bounce far with all those heavy books,' Tabitha said, and the door slammed closed.

I really did want to float to Still-Alive School, honest I did, but the thought of all those new faces—

Oh, and I'd forgotten my pencil case, and—

Anyway, my tummy told me it was time

for an early lunch, so I hid the satchel in the stinging nettles and floated over the house and in through the larder window.

I had barely eaten half a sponge cake when in floated Charlie Vapour.

'Um,' I said, wiping icing from my mouth. 'There was an earthquake, so the Still-Alive Headmaster sent us home, and the earthquake shook the shelf and the cake toppled into my mouth and—'

'Humphrey,' Charlie said as he toyed with his trilby, 'you're a big, cake-eating fibber. Wipe your mouth. I'm wisping you to Still-Alive School myself.'

Charlie's Polite Advice

Still-Alive School wasn't like our old grey Ghost School. The building was built from red bricks and had a roof as flat and boring as a maths book.

When we arrived, the still-alive children screamed at us and ran into the classrooms. The sun shone so brightly on the windows that I couldn't see in, but I knew the children were inside.

'I think I'll just float about in the playground,' I said, dragging my satchel over the railing.

'If all you do is waft about on your own,' Charlie said, 'you might as well have stayed in your room.'

I smiled when Charlie said this. 'If we leave now,' I said, 'we can be home in a float, a wisp and a flit.'

'That's not what I meant. School is about more than just the written word, Humphrey.'

'What is it about, then?'

Charlie held his hat to his chest and frowned in thought. 'School is about making girls blush behind the bike shed, and beating the school bully at conkers. At least, that's how I remember it from when I was a boy.'

'I don't want to do those things,' I said as Charlie peered at me through the railings.

'Look,' Charlie said, pointing. 'There's

another boy who's arrived late. If you float over and say hello, you might make a new friend.'

'He won't like me,' I said. 'I'm a ghost.'

'I'll hold your satchel. Off you float.'

I waited until the boy opened the door to the school building, then wisped across the playground and bumped him so hard he landed on the concrete in a heap – no fibbing!

The boy scrambled to his feet and ran out through the school gates in tears.

'Humphrey!' Charlie yelled. 'Why did you bump the poor lad?'

'To teach him a lesson for making fun of me.'

'But he didn't make fun of you,' Charlie said.

'He would have, if I hadn't bumped him.'

Charlie dragged the satchel across the playground towards me. 'If you want to get along in this world, you must learn to be polite. All it takes is a smile and a doff of the hat—'

'I don't wear a hat.'

'Bump this door open,' Charlie said, 'and I'll show you what I mean.'

Charlie left the satchel of books on the doorstep and led me along a corridor lined with shiny red doors. From behind one of the doors, we could hear a lady teacher yawning on about sums.

'Watch,' Charlie said with a wink, 'and learn.'

'Learning is what I'm here for,' I said with a gulp.

Charlie held his trilby to his chest – the polite thing to do – and passed through the wall and into the classroom.

'Forgive me for interrupting,' I heard him say, but before he could finish, the teacher

shrieked at the top of her lungs and the still-alive children made the most frightful row.

'Not quite the reaction I expected,' Charlie said, passing back.

I tugged a chocolate biscuit from my trouser pocket and took a bite. 'You see? The still-alive children are meanies, just like Wither said.'

7

Wither's Abysmal Poetry

That evening, Tabitha and Charlie had a grown-up talk in the study. I wisped into the clicky-clacky typewriter where I could watch and listen in secret.

'Humphrey used to be so popular,' Tabitha said, 'but then he started bumping.'

'He's always bumped,' Charlie said, adjusting his trilby, 'ever since he was still alive.'

'I doubt he bumped as much as he does now, Charlie.'

'I've tried talking to the boy,' Charlie said, 'but I can't get through to him.'

At that moment Wither wisped in. 'I have it!' he cried, wriggling his candlestick fingers.

'Calm down, Wither,' Tabitha said. 'Take a deep breath and tell us your idea.'

Wither took a deep breath, but when he spoke he sounded more excited than ever. 'It is as easy as algebra. If we do the still-alive pupils a good deed, they will look upon us ghosties with kindness and embrace Master Bump as a friend.'

'What do you have in mind?' Charlie said.

'If there is one thing children love,' Wither said with a smile, 'it is vegetables. And if there is one other thing children love, it is poetry.'

Charlie adjusted his tie. 'Oh, I don't know about that.'

'Tell us your plan,' said Tabitha, sounding dead kind.

'I will compose a vegetable-themed poem,' Wither announced in his warbly poetry voice, 'and recite it to the children during their English lesson.'

A moment later, Wither's fingers floated above the keys, so I wisped out of the clicky-clacky typewriter. I wanted to stay as far away from Wither's poetry as possible.

'Humphrey!' Tabitha said. 'You've been listening all this time.'

'Please don't let Wither write a poem about vegetables,' I said, trying not to blub. 'I hate vegetables, and Wither's poems are drivel.'

'Don't be mean,' said Wither.

'If Wither reads his poems at the school,' I said, 'the still-alive children will hate us ghosties more than ever.'

'Dear boy,' Wither said, 'you lack faith.'

He fed a sheet of paper into the clicky-clacky typewriter and began to type.

During the night, I could hear the click-clack of keys, and Wither wailing poetically into the darkness. 'Oh, the muse!' he wailed. 'Oh, the muse!'

When I floated into the study after breakfast, Wither lay slumped over the clicky-clacky typewriter. Agatha and Tabitha were trying to shake him awake.

'I barely slept a wink,' I said with a yawn.

'Wither,' Tabitha said, 'it's time to float to Still-Alive School and recite the poem.'

'I'm too tired to recite the, um, carrot,' Wither mumbled, prising his eyes open with his bony fingers.

'But, Wither,' Agatha said, 'you've been working on that poem all night. It would be a shame not to recite it.'

'Wake me when I'm broccoli,' Wither said,

and his haunted head flopped against the keys.

'Why did the poem take so long to write?' Tabitha asked Wither, shaking his left shoulder. 'Is it a particularly good poem?'

'It is more that it's a particularly long poem,' Wither yawned, scooping up a pile of papers. 'A twelve-thousand-page poetic epic. Come along, Humphrey. We have young minds to nurture.'

The float to school took forever. Wither kept nodding off, and every few seconds a page would sail away on the warm summer breeze and Tabitha would chase after it.

'He's fading,' I whispered to

Tabitha as the three of us wafted by the school gates.

'Wither,' Tabitha said, 'you're so tired you've turned transparent.'

'All ghosties are transparent,' Wither yawned.

'Not as transparent as that,' Tabitha said, 'and not all over. You're so see-through you're barely visible. Why not float off home and get some sleep?'

Wither shrugged, and watched lazily as

twelve thousand sheets of paper blew across the playground. 'I will have to recite my masterpiece from memory.'

The three of us flitted around the school building until we found a classroom with an open window. Inside, we could hear a lady teacher rattling on about verbs and nouns.

Wither was so tired now we could barely see him at all.

'I'll just write the poem on the whiteboard, then float off home to bed,' Wither yawned, and he wisped into the classroom.

'I doubt they'll have enough ink,' Tabitha giggled.

Tabitha and me wisped into a plant pot on the window sill and waited.

A moment later a pen lifted from the teacher's desk and scrawled the words ODE TO VEGETABLES on the whiteboard.

The teacher fainted, and the still-alive children leapt from their seats and screamed.

'At least wait until I've written the first line,' Wither's voice said, 'before you pass judgement.'

But the still-alive children were already scrambling over their desks and barging out through the classroom door.

8
Agatha's Helpful Breeze

Tabitha said I could spend the rest of the week at home, reading comics. Well, literature really, but I'd torn up my comics and hidden the pieces between the pages of Wither's books.

The comics didn't make much sense jumbled up like that, but they still made more sense than Dickens.

On Saturday, me, Tabitha, Agatha and Wither floated down to the village park.

'The still-alive children will yell mean names and run away,' I said.

'I doubt they'll be able to see us in this bright sunlight,' Agatha said.

The park was dead busy, with families sat on tartan blankets scoffing sandwiches from paper plates, and dogs chasing sticks, and nannies pushing baby still-alives in prams.

'Look at the children on the hill there,' Wither said, pointing. 'They're trying to fly kites, but there's no wind.'

'We can't have that,' Tabitha said. 'Aggie, you could create a breeze using your skills.'

'Tabitha, dearest,' Agatha said, clutching her pearls, 'with my limited abilities, I doubt I could blow the froth from a mug of coffee.'

'Modesty has its place, dear Aggie,' Wither said, 'but the boy here needs an education.'

All ghostly eyes turned to me.

'Wither,' Agatha said, 'what could you possibly mean?'

'The kite problem is nothing more than an opportunity stood upon its head.'

'What are you talking about?' Tabitha said.

'It is as simple as sums,' Wither said, and he waved his fingers like sticks of Frighten rock. 'What if Agatha were to rustle up a force-ten gale as Tabitha suggests? The still-alive children will adore us ghosties after that, the Bump boy included.'

'Me? A force-ten gale?' Agatha said with a blustery laugh. 'I can barely blow the seeds from a dandelion.'

'Rubbish,' Tabitha said. 'We've all seen the way you dry Wither's long johns.'

Wither folded his coat hanger arms. 'Agatha, the educational diet of a hungry mind is at stake.'

'My mind is the only part of me that isn't hungry,' I said. 'Anyway, what's the point in helping the still-alives? They'll only be mean to me.'

'No one is mean in the park on a Saturday,' Wither said. 'Not even the still-alive children are mean in the park on a Saturday.'

'Well, I think the plan is rotten,' I said as the four of us floated up the hillside. 'I wouldn't mind flying a kite though.'

Agatha raised a posh eyebrow at a girl holding a floppy kite. 'Now, there's a young lady who'd appreciate a gust or two.'

'Off you float then,' Tabitha said.

For a moment Agatha looked ready to flit into action, but then she shrugged, rolled her eyes, rattled her pearls and said, 'I can't do it with you three watching.'

'We'll turn the other way,' Wither said, and we did.

287

But then we turned back.

The three of us watched as Agatha wisped around the girl in a circle, once, twice, again and again and again, faster and faster, until the kite broke free of the girl's arms and lifted into the air.

'Good old Aggie!' Tabitha cried, clapping her hands.

'But she's doing it wrong,' I said. 'Look.'

Tabitha yelled at Agatha to stop, but it was too late. The kite began to spin, and the string twisted this way and that and coiled around the girl like a snake.

'Help!' the girl cried as her mother and father ran to the rescue. 'Help!'

'Stand still,' the father called, but the girl lost her balance and rolled off down the hill.

'Never mind,' Tabitha said when Agatha floated back. 'Have another go.' She squinted into the sun and pointed towards the very top of the hill. 'What about that boy there?'

The four of us floated up the hillside to where a tiny boy raced through the long grass, an orange kite held high above his head.

'A bit less round-and-round,' Agatha said to herself, 'and a lot more up-and-up.'

'We'll turn the other way,' I said, and we did.

But then we turned back.

'There she blows!' Tabitha said. 'Good old Aggie.'

The three of us watched open-mouthed as the orange kite soared high into the bright blue sky.

'Isn't Agatha wisping a bit fast?' I said.

'You're right,' Wither said. 'The poor still-alive is struggling to keep up.'

Tabitha gasped as the boy's trainers lifted from the ground. Up and up he went, gripping the wooden reel with his fingers.

'The kite is carrying him away,' I said. 'Why doesn't he let go?'

'It's too late for that,' Wither said. 'If he hits the ground from that height, he'll turn into one of us.'

The other still-alives stopped scoffing sandwiches and pushing prams and throwing sticks for dogs, and ran after the terrified, tiny boy. Perhaps they thought they'd be able to catch him if he let go of the reel.

'Help!' the boy cried. 'Help! Help!'

'We have to get him down!' one of the still-alives yelled.

'He'll bump his head on an aeroplane!' yelled another.

'And what if he's pecked by birds!' yelled another.

Whenever the boy bobbed beneath the clouds, the still-alives ran towards him, but then he'd disappear out of sight and reappear

somewhere else, and the still-alives would have to run in a different direction.

Then a gust of wind sent the boy sailing off to the east, and the still-alives ran out through the park gates, dogs yapping at their heels.

We floated around for a bit, then Agatha said, 'We might as well enjoy ourselves, while we're here.' And she wisped off over the hill.

'Where's she gone?' I said, and Wither and Tabitha shrugged.

When Agatha floated back a minute later, she held four ghostly raspberry-ripple I-screams.

'Good old Aggie,' Tabitha said, and we gave our I-screams a joyful lick.

As we floated home through the village later that afternoon, we came across a crowd of still-alives gathered on the pavement by the church.

'Today must be Sunday,' Wither said.

'It can't be,' Tabitha said. 'It was Saturday when we left the house.'

We floated closer. The still-alives were gawping at a boy bound to the church spire, an orange kite dangling from his ankle.

Several newspaper reporters were taking photographs and scrawling in their notepads. A policeman propped a ladder against the church wall, but it barely reached the roof.

Two minutes later, the crowd parted as a fire engine roared down the street, sounding its siren.

'What a brave little boy,' Agatha said, and we wisped off home.

9
Humphrey's
New Friend

Whatever the grown-up ghosties did, nothing
seemed to help.

On Monday I floated to Still-Alive School
alone. When I peered through the railings I saw
two still-alive boys teasing a girl.

'Fatty-Fatty Pigtails!' the boys yelled.
'Fatty-Fatty Pigtails!'

'I'm not fat,' the girl said, rubbing her

round tummy. 'And these aren't pigtails. They're plaits.'

She started to blub, and the boys laughed.

I felt a funny feeling in my tummy. Not the funny feeling I get when I've eaten candyfloss on toast. No, this was an angry feeling.

I wisped over the railing and bumped the two boys to the ground.

The girl screamed.

'I'm sorry,' I said. 'I didn't mean to scare you.'

The girl dried her eyes and peered at me through her glasses. 'You rescued me.'

'Yes,' I said.

'I'm ever so grateful. But you're – you're see-through, and you float.'

'I'm a ghost,' I said, 'a real live ghost.' I pinched myself, then added, 'Well, a real dead ghost.'

'You're not like the ghosts in films. You have a friendly face.'

'Oh, I'm frightfully friendly,' I said, and I wriggled my transparent bits.

The girl tugged her plaits. 'I have to go now, or I'll be in trouble.'

'All right,' I said. 'My name is Humphrey, by the way. Humphrey Bump.'

'I can see why they call you Bump,' the girl said, glancing at the two bruised boys. 'My name is Amelia. I have to run now, or I'll be late for maths.'

When I arrived home I found the girl ghosties baking cakes in the kitchen. Wither floated above the stove reading a spooky cookery book.

'You look happy,' Tabitha said.

'I had a good day at Still-Alive School,' I said, dumping my satchel on the kitchen table.

'Rather a short good day,' Wither said,

checking the time on his pocket watch. 'School begins at nine o'clock sharp. It is barely a minute after ten.'

'At least he went,' Agatha said. 'Humphrey, tell us what happened.'

'I made friends with a still-alive girl,' I said, grabbing a handful of cherries.

Wither frowned. 'But the still-alive children are meanies.'

'Not once you get to know them.'

'You should float to school again this afternoon,' Tabitha said, 'before your new friend forgets who you are.'

'I'll do that,' I said, and I did.

The trouble was, when I arrived at Still-Alive School there were so many children in the playground I thought I'd never find her.

'Amelia?' I yelled. 'Is anyone friends with Amelia?'

Wherever I floated, children yelled mean things and ran away.

I'd almost given up when a familiar voice called out from a group of girl still-alives. I smiled a smile as big as a slice of raspberry pie. 'Amelia!'

'Humphrey,' Amelia said, glancing round at her fleeing friends, 'I can't be friends with you. I'm sorry.'

'Oh,' I said, trying not to blub. 'Well, I just thought you might like to share this chocolate bar. It's ghost chocolate, so you won't be able to eat it, but—'

'This is why we can't be friends,' Amelia said. 'You're a ghost, and I'm still alive.'

'I wish I was still alive too,' I said, and I wisped off.

10

Eggs, Bacon and Porridge

'I may be round,' I muttered as I rolled out of bed the next morning, 'but I'm no quitter.'

Charlie passed his head through the bedroom door. 'Talking to yourself, Humphrey Bump?'

'Knock before you pass through,' I said. 'It's the polite thing to do, and I might be getting dressed.'

'I tried knocking,' Charlie said, 'but it's rather a thin door and my knuckles passed through the wood.'

At breakfast, the grown-up ghosties asked me about my new friend.

'Is she pretty?' Charlie said, prising the lid from the marmalade jar.

Wither cracked the shell of a boiled egg. 'Charlie, for one so polite, you possess frightfully poor manners.'

'Is she charming?' Pamela asked as she buttered the ghostly toast.

'Oh, and is she a swot?' Agatha said. 'I mean, is she clever?'

I didn't say anything.

'At least tell us your new girlfriend's name,' Agatha said, and she blew the steam from her porridge.

'Her name is Amelia,' I mumbled into my bacon and eggs, 'but she isn't my—'

'Just good friends,' Tabitha said with a wink.

'That wasn't what I meant. When I talked to Amelia in the playground yesterday afternoon, she said she can't be friends with a ghosty.'

'Oh, the meanness!' cried Wither, and he dunked a soldier into his egg yolk.

'Let's face it,' Charlie said, 'Still-Alive School just isn't ready for a phantom pupil.'

The grown-up ghosties peered at me over their plates and bowls, and I felt like wisping off to my room and hiding under the bed.

Then Charlie lifted his hat from the table, flicked a crumb from the brim, and placed the hat on his head. 'Except that Humphrey isn't a quitter. Isn't that right, Humphrey?'

I thought back to how brave I'd felt earlier that morning, when I rolled out of bed. 'It's time I packed my satchel,' I said, and I floated out to the hall.

'Good on you, Humphrey,' Tabitha said.

'What about your breakfast?' Charlie called.

'I want to arrive early,' I called back, 'while there aren't too many still-alives about.'

When I wisped down the ornate staircase, my school tie wafting behind me, I found Tabitha, Charlie, Wither, Agatha and Pamela floating by the front door.

'We thought we'd come with you,' Agatha said. 'If we put our haunted heads together—'

Tabitha clapped her hands, and the front door creaked open.

'I need to solve this problem for myself,' I said as the six of us floated out of the house.

'How mean,' said Wither, and he pursed his lips.

When I looked round, the grown-up ghosties had gone.

11

Bumping Lessons

As I floated across the empty playground, past the prickly bushes decorated with crisp packets and flowers, an idea struck.

My idea was that I'd wisp into one of the classrooms, find a seat at the back, and float above it doing sums. By the time the lesson started, the still-alives would be used to my ghostly presence, and they wouldn't be mean to me.

That's what it's called when there's a ghost

in the room. A ghostly presence.
Wither told me
that, and Wither
is a poet.

I found a
classroom with an
open window and
floated in.

When I opened
my spooky satchel,
five frightfully
friendly ghosties
wisped out.

'We're here to
help you make
friends,' Agatha said.

'It was my idea,' Charlie said, and he
held his hat to his chest.

'Charlie, don't boast,' Agatha said. 'It's
hardly the polite thing to do.'

'I did doff my trilby, Agatha.'

'Anyway,' Pamela said, hiding her eyes, 'it was my idea, not Charlie Vapour's.'

Wither folded his bony arms. 'But I was the first ghosty to wisp into Humphrey's satchel.'

'I'm sure we all thought of it together,' Tabitha said.

'Well,' I said, 'I don't care who thought of it. The idea stinks.'

The school bell buzzed, and Pamela screamed.

'What a frightful noise,' Agatha said, and she plugged her ears with her fingers.

'It's time for lessons to start,' I said, 'and you grown-up ghosties have ruined everything.'

'But we came to help,' Tabitha said.

'I don't need your help. I just want the still-alive children to like me. If they see you lot, they'll hate me more than ever.'

The classroom door opened, and a still-alive girl walked in. When she saw six frightfully friendly ghosties, she screamed and ran off down the corridor.

'Told you,' I said, and I blew a raspberry.

Wither held a bony finger to his lips. 'Shh! Listen!'

We listened.

'Fatty-Fatty Pigtails! Fatty-Fatty Pigtails!' a voice called.

We turned to the window, and could just make out three figures on the other side of the prickly hedge.

'That's Amelia,' I said. 'Those two boys are bullies.'

'You should bump them,' Charlie said with a wink.

'Amelia will certainly want to be friends if you rescue her from bullies,' Tabitha said.

'I've already tried that.'

'Then bump them again,' said Wither. 'Some bullies need bumping twice.'

'Teach them a lesson!' Charlie yelled as I wisped out through the open window.

As I floated over the prickly hedge, another idea struck. I knew I couldn't protect Amelia forever. Perhaps I could teach her to protect herself.

I wisped into Amelia's left ear and whispered, 'Bump them.'

'Humphrey,' Amelia said, 'is that you?'

'Yes,' I whispered. 'Amelia, you have a round tummy, like me. Put it to good use and bump the bullies into the hedge.'

'I couldn't, Humphrey. I'd get into trouble with the Headmaster.'

Another idea struck, the third I'd had that day. I wisped out of Amelia's left ear, took a deep breath and bumped poor Amelia, sending her bouncing into the two boys, who landed upside down in the prickly hedge.

Inside the classroom, the five grown-up ghosties cheered.

'Humphrey,' Amelia said, brushing gravel from her knees, 'we bumped the bullies.'

'Next time you're bullied, you'll know what to do,' I said, and I floated off, leaving Amelia smiling proudly.

12
The Still-Alive Headmaster

'I'm glad we decided to be friends,' Amelia said that afternoon. 'School playtimes can be fun now.'

We sat together on a bench at the edge of the playground. Well, Amelia sat, and I floated.

'I can eat my ordinary crisps,' Amelia said as she crunched, 'and you can eat your ghost crisps, and—'

'But, Amelia, you're crying.'

'School is horrid,' Amelia said, and she blew her nose on her left plait.

'It needn't be, now that we're friends.'

Amelia shook her head. 'There will always be bullying in this world, Humphrey, no matter who you're friends with.'

'Bump them, like how I taught you.'

'There are some bullies who just can't be bumped.'

'I'm not afraid of any bully,' I said, and I munched another creepy crisp.

Amelia frowned, then looked at me and said, 'You'd be afraid of this bully.'

'Why? Who is he?'

'The Headmaster.'

I laughed, spilling crisps down my blazer. 'I bumped the Ghost Headmaster at Ghost School. No one bullies Humphrey Bump.'

'Didn't you get into trouble?'

'He'd already expelled me,' I explained. 'That's why I'm here, at Still-Alive School.'

'Humphrey, I can't get expelled. I'm top of the class in science. I plan to go to university.'

'Then you'd better stay out of his way,' I said, opening another bag of crisps.

'I can't,' Amelia said, and she began to cry again. 'I have to see the Headmaster today after school.'

'But why?'

Amelia sniffed into her crisp packet, and said, 'For bumping bullies.'

At last bell, I floated in through the window of the Still-Alive Headmaster's office and wisped behind the potted plant.

As I peered out between the dusty green leaves, I heard a faint phantom blub.

'Wither,' I whispered, 'is that you?'

'I'm hiding in the hem of the curtain,' Wither blubbed. 'I wisped in, and now I can't wisp out.'

'What do you mean, you can't wisp out?'

'The Still-Alive Headmaster is mean,' Wither blubbed.

'You don't get to be a headmaster without being mean, Wither.'

'This headmaster is so mean he makes other headmasters seem scarcely mean at all.'

'But, Wither, why did you float into the Still-Alive Headmaster's office in the first place?'

'I wanted to see how mean he was,' Wither said, and he blubbed.

The office door opened, and a girl walked in.

'Humphrey,' Wither sniffed, 'that girl looks familiar.'

'She's my still-alive friend, Amelia,' I whispered. 'Amelia has been sent to the Headmaster for bumping bullies into the hedge.'

'That's triple mean,' Wither blubbed. 'The bullies were mean to Amelia, then Amelia was

mean to the bullies, and now the Still-Alive
Headmaster—'

'Keep quiet,' I whispered. 'I want to hear
what he says.'

From my hiding place behind the leaves of
the potted plant, I could just make out the Still-
Alive Headmaster sat at his desk, and Amelia
nervously biting her fingernails.

'Well?' the Still-Alive Headmaster yelled.
'What do you have to say for yourself, child?'

'I'm sorry, sir,' Amelia said. 'Um, it won't
happen again, and—'

'Not good enough, child!' the Headmaster
yelled, his face the colour of beetroot.

Amelia backed away as the Still-Alive
Headmaster stood from his chair and leant
towards her across the desk, jabbing the air
with a spiny finger.

'Lines!' the Still-Alive Headmaster yelled.
'Ten thousand, in your neatest handwriting.

Fifty hours litter duty. And two hours detention each day for a month.'

'Oh, the meanness!' Wither blubbed, and he wisped up from the hem of the curtain and floated out through the office window.

For a moment the Still-Alive Headmaster looked almost afraid. 'What in heaven's name was that?'

'A friend of a friend,' Amelia said, and she walked out of the Headmaster's office with a smile.

13
Who's Afraid of Humphrey Bump?

'Haven't you noticed,' Amelia whispered on Wednesday afternoon, 'how unhappy everyone is?'

'I'm sure they'd rather be out riding their bicycles in the sun,' I said, peering out from Amelia's satchel. 'Anything other than opening their maths books.'

'That's not what I meant.' Amelia

Z Z Z Z Z Z z z z z

sat at her desk and lowered the satchel to the floor. 'School days are supposed to be the best days of your life. Ever since this new headmaster arrived last term, I've not seen one cheerful face.'

I broke a chunk from a ghostly chocolate bar and popped it into my mouth.

'And look at how tired everyone is, Humphrey.'

I peered out of the satchel and glanced around the classroom. Two of the boys had their heads in their arms. One girl was snoring loudly. 'They stayed up late watching cartoons, I guess.'

'Cartoons? Humphrey, after a day of lessons, followed by five hours of homework, I doubt they can keep their eyes open.'

'Five hours of homework?'

'Headmaster's rules,' Amelia whispered.

The room fell silent as the Still-Alive

Headmaster strode in on his long, mean legs. He glanced around the classroom, then pointed at a boy in the front row. 'You, child, where is the teacher?'

'You – you fired her, sir,' the boy stammered.

'Raise your hand when you speak, child,' the Headmaster yelled, and the boy raised his hand. 'You're expelled. Gather your pencils, child, and get out.'

'You can't expel a boy for forgetting to raise his hand,' I whispered.

'We're lucky he's in a good mood,' Amelia whispered back, 'or he'd have expelled the entire class.'

'He can't do that!'

'It's happened before, Humphrey. I told you the headmaster was a bully.'

'Well, it's got to stop,' I said.

'Humphrey,' Amelia gasped, 'what are you going to do?'

'You've heard of things that go bump in the night? Well, I'm going to go bump in the daytime, right here in this maths room.'

'You'll get yourself into trouble.'

I loosened my school tie. 'What can he do, expel me?'

'Just be careful, Humphrey.'

'He's the one who should be careful,' I said, and I wisped out from Amelia's satchel. The still-alive children screamed and ran out of the classroom, and the Still-Alive Headmaster backed into the corner. I took a deep breath and gave the Still-Alive Headmaster the bumpiest bump I'd ever bumped.

'Ghostly child,' the Headmaster said, straightening his hairpiece, 'surely you can bump me better than that?'

'How do you mean?'

'Must try harder,' the Still-Alive Headmaster said, and he walked out of the classroom.

'But that was my best-ever bump,' I said, tugging a jam doughnut from my blazer pocket. I'd intended to bump him again, but somehow I'd lost heart.

'Perhaps you don't need to bump him,' Amelia said from the doorway. 'You're a ghost, Humphrey. Most people find ghosts terrifying.'

'I'd forgotten about that,' I said, and I wisped off down the corridor, wriggling my transparent bits and pulling a mean face.

The Still-Alive Headmaster just stood there shaking his head – pitifully, I think.

'I'm a ghost,' I said. 'Aren't you afraid?'

'Not in the least,' the Still-Alive Headmaster said, and he walked off.

14

Humphrey's Speech

Thursday morning, as I floated across the field to Still-Alive School, I bumped into Wither.

'I thought you'd stopped all that bumping nonsense,' Wither said.

'Sorry.'

I told Wither about what had happened with the Still-Alive Headmaster in the maths room.

'Some still-alives are afraid of ghosties,' I said, 'but not this still-alive. I wriggled my transparent bits and he didn't bat an eyelid.'

Wither rubbed his chin. 'And you bumped him, you say?'

'Left, right and centre,' I said, picking an apple from a nearby apple tree.

'He must be afraid of something. Every still-alive is afraid of something.'

'Well,' I said, 'he did look afraid when you wisped out from his curtains. Only for a moment, then he sort of pulled himself together.'

'Hmm,' Wither said. 'It seems to me that this mean-spirited still-alive is indeed afraid of ghosties, but only a bit.'

'What are you getting at?' I said, crunching the rosy apple.

'It's like this. Let's say I've just penned a quite-good poem. If I wish to lift the poem to greatness, I simply write a further two hundred verses.'

'But that makes the poem worse,' I said.

'Your poetry is drivel. The less of it there is, the better.'

Wither didn't seem to hear. I think he was lost in a poetic reverie or something.

I tossed the half-eaten apple into a hedge. 'Wither, I know you're trying to help—'

'Allow me to finish,' Wither said. 'If this headmaster is afraid of one ghosty a bit, he will be afraid of a lot of ghosties a lot.'

I thought about this for a moment, then said, 'That actually makes sense.'

'Let's see.' Wither held up his knitting-needle fingers and began to count. 'There's myself, you and I – that's three. And the three girl ghosties makes six. And then there's Charlie. And Humphrey – that's you – which makes eight—'

'Shh,' I said. 'Listen.'

Wither cupped his ear with his hand. 'But, Humphrey, you're not saying anything.'

'Not to me. To, um, everything else.'

We listened.

Wither said, 'I can't hear anything. Well, only the ghost children at Ghost School across the field there, but—'

'Wait here,' I said, and I flitted across the field and over the high grey wall and into the Ghost School playground.

After a quick float around, I spotted Samuel Spook floating by the bike shed.

We used to be good friends, but when I wafted across the playground towards him he turned up his nose.

'Samuel,' I said, 'I need your help. There's this headmaster at Still-Alive School, and—'

'I can't hear you,' Samuel said, and he poked his fingers into his ears.

'But, Samuel, we're friends.'

'After you bumped me into the sausage trolley in the canteen?'

'I'd forgotten about that.'

'Fight your own battles,' Samuel said, and he floated off.

Just as I felt ready to give up and wisp back to Wither, I spotted the terrifying twins, Phil and Fay Phantom.

When I floated over, Fay folded her arms, and Phil looked through his shoes.

'I need your help,' I said. 'There's this headmaster—'

'You've got a nerve,' Phil said.

'You bumped me into the swimming pool,' Fay said, and she tossed her hair.

'Only in fun, Fay.'

327

'And you bumped me down the stairs,' Phil said. 'If I wasn't dead, I might've been hurt.'

'I can explain.'

'Don't bother,' the twins said together, and off they wisped.

I floated, slowly, back over the high grey wall and across the field to where Wither wafted poetically beneath the leaves of a sycamore tree.

'Humphrey, you look like you've found a cupcake and dropped it.'

I explained how the ghost children refused to help, and about how they hated me because I'd bumped them.

'What you must do,' Wither said, 'is return to Ghost School and move the children to tears with a heartfelt speech. The children will flock to your cause like moths to a flame.'

'I'm no good with words, Wither.'

'I'll wisp back to the house,' Wither said,

chewing a wasp, 'and write a speech on the clicky-clacky typewriter.'

'If you don't mind, I'd rather make it up as I go along.'

Together we floated across the field, higher this time, so high that the sheep and trees and the Ghost School building looked like toys.

I floated down, waving my arms above my head. The children gathered round to hear what I had to say.

'I'm sorry for bumping you. I just wanted to have fun, that's all.'

'Boo!' the children booed. 'Boo! Boo!'

'Please listen,' I said. 'There's this headmaster at Still-Alive School, and he's a bully, and, um—'

'Boo! Boo!'

'Look,' I said, 'if you don't help me, I won't have a school to go to, and I'll have to study at home with Wither.'

'The boring old Victorian poet?' Phil Phantom said.

'That's what you get for bumping us,' Samuel Spook said.

I shrugged, bit into a jam doughnut and wisped off.

15
Crime and
Punishment

I found Amelia in the corridor, outside the Still-Alive Headmaster's office.

'Humphrey,' Amelia said, 'something terrible has happened.'

'What?'

'The Headmaster heard the bullies calling me names. He's given them lines. One million each, in their best handwriting.'

I shrugged.

'It's wrong,' Amelia said. 'The punishment should fit the crime, don't you think?'

We peered into the office. The Still-Alive Headmaster was standing between the two boys and the open door.

'We can't write a million lines,' one of the bullies said.

The Still-Alive Headmaster folded his arms. 'You're not leaving my office until you do.'

'We've got to get them out of there,' I whispered.

'Bump him,' Amelia whispered back.

'I don't think I can,' I groaned, holding my tummy. 'I've just eaten twelve jam doughnuts.'

'If you don't bump him,' Amelia whispered, 'I will.'

'You'll get expelled, and you won't be able to go to university.' I reached out to stop her but my hand passed right through. When I feel queasy, I tend to fade a bit.

Amelia took a deep breath and bumped the Headmaster's bottom.

The two boys exchanged looks. 'It's Fatty-Fatty Pigtails,' one of them said as they slipped past the Still-Alive Headmaster.

'Um, I don't think we should call her that,' the other boy said. 'That girl just saved our bacon.'

'You are both expelled!' the Headmaster yelled, but the boys ran off up the corridor and out into the playground.

We followed the Still-Alive Headmaster as he strode through the school grounds, pointing at still-alive children with a long, mean finger.

'Expelled!' he yelled. 'Expelled, expelled, expelled!'

Amelia gasped.

'That's right,' he said, fixing his eyes on Amelia. 'I am expelling every pupil in this school.'

16
The Headmaster's Wife

On Friday morning a crowd of still-alive children gathered at the school gates. I didn't want them to see me, so I flitted round to the back of the school and wisped over the fence.

'I'm glad you're here, Humphrey,' Amelia said when we met in the back playground. 'Something big is happening, and I need your help.'

'I didn't think anyone would be here,' I said. 'I thought you'd all been expelled.'

'Not yet. The Headmaster has to fill in forms and write to the parents.'

'That Headmaster is so mean,' I said, 'he'll do it, even if it takes him all night,'

Amelia smiled. 'He'll have to get into his office first.'

I followed Amelia to the main entrance. Two boys blocked our path.

'Friend or foe?' one of the boys barked.

The boys wore scout caps pulled down over their eyes. Each had a badge taped to his blazer, just below the left shoulder. SECURITY, the badges read.

'It's me – Amelia. If you pulled your caps up you'd be able to see properly.'

The boys lifted their caps, and I recognised them as the bullies. 'Oh, hello,' they both said together.

'They've been good as gold since I rescued them from the Headmaster,' Amelia told me. 'I've put them in charge of security.'

One of the boys opened the door and gestured for us to step inside.

'Amelia,' I said as I followed her down the corridor, 'what's happening?'

'We've taken over the school. The Headmaster can't expel us if he's not in charge.'

I opened a can of fizzy pop.

'And it's not just here,' Amelia went on. 'Every school in the country has put down their pencils, kicked back their chairs and made a stand.'

'That's not a good idea,' I said. 'When the Headmaster hears of this—'

'He won't be able to do a thing. Look.'

The door to the Headmaster's office had been sealed shut with pink stuff.

'Bubble gum,' Amelia said. She took my haunted hand and said, 'Come on.'

'Where are we going now?'

Amelia led me out into the front playground. The air buzzed with cheers and jeers.

'This has got out of hand,' I said.

'What choice is there?' Amelia said. 'After all, if we let the Headmaster into his office, we'll all be expelled.'

'Where is the Headmaster now?'

We heard the screech of car brakes, and Amelia ran across the playground to the railings. I floated up into the air for a better view.

The Still-Alive Headmaster had parked his car right outside the gates. He opened the driver's door and stepped onto the pavement.

'Headmaster, Headmaster, you're so mean!' the children chanted. 'The meanest headmaster we've ever seen!'

'Children,' the Still-Alive Headmaster said, 'go home, or you will be arrested by the police.'

I flitted down and floated at Amelia's side. 'The police would sooner arrest him than you lot,' I told her.

'I'm not so sure. The Police Chief is the Headmaster's wife.'

The Still-Alive Headmaster tried to walk through the gates, but the still-alive pupils linked arms and jostled about.

Several police cars and police vans pulled up, their lights flashing, their sirens wailing. The police officers leapt out, buttoning their tunics and fastening the straps on their helmets.

'That must be the Headmaster's wife,' Amelia said, pointing at a fierce-looking woman in a peaked cap.

'Children,' the woman yelled through a loudhailer, 'place your hands on your heads. You are all under arrest.'

'You can't arrest us!' the children cried. 'We're children!'

'I'll get my dad onto you,' one boy shouted.

Nothing the still-alive boys and girls could say did any good. The Police Chief blew her whistle, and the police officers grabbed the children by the arms and led them back to the police vehicles.

'We have to do something,' I said, but Amelia just shrugged.

'There's nothing we can do, Humphrey. We can't resist the entire police force.'

'Perhaps I can frighten them,' I said, and I wisped across the road, poked out my tongue and blew a raspberry.

The police officers and the children screamed, but the Still-Alive Headmaster just laughed. 'That,' he yelled, pointing at me with his mean finger, 'is nothing but a trick of the light.'

Amelia stepped out through the gates with her hands on her head. 'It's no use,' she told me. 'We might as well give ourselves up.'

'Never,' I said, and I bumped the Still-Alive Headmaster into his wife.

'There,' I said, winking at Amelia. 'That should shut them up.'

'I doubt it, Humphrey. It's like I said. There are some bullies you just can't bump.'

The Still-Alive Headmaster helped the Police Chief to her feet. 'Spectral child,' he said, 'you can bump my wife and me till the cows come home. We're not going to believe in you, and that's that.'

Then something odd happened.

The colour drained from his wife's face, and her eyes bulged like globes.

'Mildred, my dear,' the Still-Alive Headmaster said, 'whatever is the matter? You look like you've seen a—'

'Jonathan,' his wife said, 'look!'

The Still-Alive Headmaster turned, following his wife's gaze. When he saw the sight of a blue summer sky swarming with ghostly schoolchildren, he almost leapt out of his skin. 'What in heaven's name—'

The police woman who'd been holding Amelia by the wrist let go and leapt into a hedge.

'Humphrey,' Amelia gasped, 'who are they? What's going on?'

'Oh, just some friends of mine,' I said, and I smiled.

Phantom children from all of history had come to join the fight against bullying. Ghostly girls in Victorian pinnies skipped across the rooftops with spooky skipping ropes, or played hopscotch in the clouds. Ghostly boys in short trousers, blazers and caps kicked phantom footballs or skidded through the sky on transparent bikes.

'Wonderful!' Amelia cried, clapping her hands.

'I asked the children at Ghost School to help us,' I said, 'and, um, here they are, um, helping!'

The two of us watched as the ghost children wisped around the vans and cars, pressing their frightening faces against the windows. 'Let the children go!' they wailed. 'Set the children free!'

The police officers did what they were told, and the still-alive children laughed and cheered as they stepped back onto the pavement.

As for the schoolteachers and dinner ladies, the meaner ones fled, and the kind ones stayed to greet their new supernatural friends.

'It's time we had a word with the Headmaster,' I said. 'Um, Amelia?'

'That,' Amelia said, 'is the most beautiful sight I have ever seen.'

'Amelia, we have to talk to the

Headmaster, before he decides he dreamt the whole thing.'

The air was so thick with ghosties we couldn't see him at first, but then Amelia spotted him trying to climb over the wall of a nearby garden.

'Not so fast,' I said. 'Amelia has something to say, and you'd better listen, or we'll haunt you for the rest of your life.'

The Still-Alive Headmaster lowered himself to the pavement, and stood with his back to the garden wall.

'You're nothing but an overgrown bully,' I said, and I opened another can of fizzy pop.

'This school,' Amelia said, pointing at the red-brick building, 'deserves a headmaster who cares about the pupils. We demand that you resign and promise us that you will never work in education again.'

'No!' the Still-Alive Headmaster cried, and

he pulled his hairpiece down over his eyes. 'This cannot be!'

The Still-Alive Headmaster stumbled away from the wall and into the arms of his wife, and the ghost children wisped around them in a circle, faster and faster, flitting this way and that as they called the Headmaster's name. 'Jonathan!' they called. 'Jonathan! Quit your job or stop being mean!'

'Let me go!' the Still-Alive Headmaster cried. 'I'll do anything. Just leave me in peace.'

'If we let you go,' I said, 'do you promise to do all you can to ensure that this school gets the head teacher it deserves?'

'I promise!' the Still-Alive Headmaster bawled, and he sprinted off down the street, his wife following close behind.

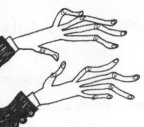

17
The Last Laugh

On Monday, as the still-alive pupils filed
into assembly, I wisped into Amelia's
satchel. I wanted to hear the new Still-Alive
Headmaster's introductory speech.

'You don't need to hide any more,
Humphrey,' Amelia said in the corridor.

'There isn't room in this school for a
phantom pupil,' I said. 'I think it's best I keep
out of sight.'

'You're right,' Amelia whispered. 'The sooner

this school gets back to normal, the
better.'

'Amelia, have you seen Humphrey
Bump?' a vaporous voice said, and I wisped
out of the satchel to find Samuel Spook
floating by the assembly-hall door. 'Ah,
Humphrey!'

'Samuel,' I said, glancing round at the
frightened faces, 'I think we'd better keep out
of sight. The sooner this school gets back to
normal, the better.'

'Good idea,' Samuel said, and the two of us
wisped into Amelia's satchel.

But then we heard a girl's voice say, 'Anyone
seen Humphrey?'

'He's in my satchel,' Amelia said, opening
the flap.

'Fay and Phil,' I said, peering out. 'Samuel
and I are trying to keep out of sight.'

'The sooner this school gets back to normal,

the better.' Samuel told the Phantom twins as they wisped in.

Amelia followed the other pupils into the hall. 'The old headmaster promised he'd find us a decent head teacher,' she whispered. 'Let's hope he's kept his word.'

'No one can be as bad as that mean-spirited bully,' I whispered back.

But when the new headmaster took to the stage, we had the shock of our lives.

The new headmaster was Wither.

'Hush, please!' Wither wailed, waving his willowy arms. 'Remain quiet, or you won't be able to hear my poem.'

I wisped out of Amelia's satchel, followed by Samuel and the twins.

'Oh, what have we done?' Amelia said.

I shrugged. 'It looks like that old bully has had the last laugh after all.'

Amelia looked at me and smiled. 'Wither's poetry can't be that bad. Um, can it?'

'It's worse than bad,' Samuel said, and the twins laughed.

'Put these in your ears,' I said, and I handed Amelia two strawberry marshmallows.

An interview with Daren King

Who is your favourite ghostie?
Charlie Vapour. Like me, he's dapper and he looks
good in a trilby.

Where do you normally write your stories?
At the funfair, on the rollercoaster. When it's raining I
write at home.

What is your favourite colour?
Orange. No, blue. Wait . . . no, red. Definitely red.

Are you scared of the dark?
I find darkness comforting. It's like a warm, soft
duvet.

Have you ever seen a ghost?
I've seen hundreds of ghosts, and all were frightfully
friendly.

Where do you get your ideas from?
Most of my ideas come from conversations. If you
talk about fun things with your friends, you will have
fun ideas.

What is the worst job you've ever had?
I used to work as a secret agent. I was terrible at it.
The problem was, I just can't keep a secret.

An interview with David Roberts

Who is your favourite ghostie?
My favourite ghostie to draw is Rusty Chains because of his clanking chains and his miserable face.

When did you start to draw?
I have always loved drawing. When I was very small my favourite things to draw were ladies wearing big dresses.

What is your favourite colour?
My favourite colour is grey because there are so many different shades. My second favourite colour is yellow.

Are you scared of the dark?
I thought I wasn't scared of the dark until a few years ago in the Welsh countryside; there were no street lights and I had to walk through woods to get to my holiday cottage. It was so dark I could not even see my feet. There were creepy sounds all around me and I was TERRIFIED.

Have you ever seen a ghost?
No. I am very pleased to say that I haven't!

Ahoy there!

There's more frightfully friendly fun in

Frightfully Friendly Ghosties:
Phantom Pirates

Join Pamela Fraidy, Humphrey Bump and the rest of the gang in this spooky new adventure on the high seas!